"I don't want to take you!"

Rick drew a ragged breath. "When I take a woman to my bed I want exactly that—a woman." He looked her over disdainfully. "Maybe in a couple of years you'll qualify."

The pain he was deliberately inflicting filled her eyes, her senses still alive from his fierce kisses. "But you want me; you said you did!"

Rick's tone was grim. "I'd want any attractive willing female at the moment."

"You mean you—" Robyn licked dry lips "—you just want me because I'm here and—and willing?"

His mouth twisted, his appraisal insulting. "You are, aren't you?"

"I was," she corrected quietly, suddenly feeling numb. How could she love this man?

CAROLE MORTIMER
is also the author of these

Harlequin Presents

Many of these titles are available at your local bookseller.

For a free catalogue listing all available Harlequin Romances
and Harlequin Presents, send your name and address to:

HARLEQUIN READER SERVICE
1440 South Priest Drive, Tempe, AZ 85281
Canadian address: Stratford, Ontario N5A 6W2

CAROLE MORTIMER

shadowed stranger

Harlequin Books

TORONTO • LONDON • LOS ANGELES • AMSTERDAM
SYDNEY • HAMBURG • PARIS • STOCKHOLM • ATHENS • TOKYO

For
John and Matthew

———————————◆◆◆———————————

Harlequin Presents first edition September 1982
ISBN 0-373-10531-2

Original hardcover edition published in 1982
by Mills & Boon Limited

CHAPTER ONE

TREES overshadowed the narrow lane she was riding down, and several large holes in the road made her bicycle wobble precariously. Birds were singing in those trees, the sound of children laughing happily as they played in the brilliant sunshine.

Children laughing . . .? There shouldn't be any children laughing here. The only house in this area, at the end of this small country lane, was Orchard House, and it had been unoccupied for quite some time now. She knew that some of the village children played there, but if Billy were one of them . . .

Yes, there he was, right in the middle of a crowd of other youngsters, the game of five-a-side football obviously well under way, sweaters being placed on the ground as goalposts.

Robyn came to a halt, straddling her bicycle. Her brother was enjoying the game; for some reason she couldn't see, football was an obsession with him and his impish face was alive with glee as he scored a goal through the makeshift goalposts.

'Billy?' she called to him. 'Billy!' more firmly as he seemed not to hear her.

He looked up impatiently. The two of them were very much alike, both blond and fair-skinned, although Billy's manner was the more aggressive. 'What is it?' he asked impatiently.

'You know you shouldn't be in here.' She felt rather silly now, the other boys were looking at her as if she had no right to be here. And maybe she didn't, but neither did they! Billy had already been in trouble with her father once about trespassing into the grounds at

Orchard House, and if he were caught again he would
be in real trouble.

'Stop interfering!' her brother snapped, obviously
embarrassed at her bossy attitude in front of his friends.

'This is private property,' she told them all firmly.
'The last time Constable Fuller caught you he gave you
all a warning, the next time it might be rather more
serious.' Especially for Billy. Her parents had been so
shocked and upset when the local policeman had called
at the house to tell them of Billy's trespassing.

'Robyn——'

'I'm sorry, Billy,' she said, and meant it. 'But I think
you should play football somewhere else.'

'There isn't anywhere else,' he snapped.

'Well, you can't stay here—any of you,' she added
meaningly.

The other boys started to wander off, shooting her
resentful glances as they went. She felt awful for spoiling
their fun, but if she had heard them there was a fair
chance Constable Fuller would too if he should go by,
and she knew for a fact that most of these boys would
be in as much trouble as Billy if they were caught here
again.

'I bet you're great at a party,' Billy muttered once
there was just the two of them left.

Robyn sighed. 'I did it for your own good.'

'That's what Dad always says before he keeps me in
or stops my pocket-money.' He kicked moodily at some
of the stones on the driveway.

'I'm sorry, Billy,' she told him ruefully. 'I didn't mean
to break up your game. Am I forgiven?'

He seemed to think about it for a while, but she knew
he would soon get over his mood—he always did.
'Okay,' he finally accepted. 'But help me look for my
football first. It had just been kicked into that long grass
among those trees when you interrupted us.'

'All right,' she agreed cheerfully, leaving her bicycle on the side of the gravel driveway of the house as they went to find the ball.

The grass was almost up to their knees, the ball nowhere in sight. But there were lots of wild daffodils growing in the grass, and Robyn couldn't resist picking some of them.

'That's called stealing!' Billy appeared at her side with his football.

'I know, but——' Just at that moment a car turned into the driveway, the wheels going over Robyn's bicycle with a telling crunch of metal. The car came to an immediate halt.

Robyn's instant reaction was to duck behind a wide tree trunk, pulling the suddenly immobile Billy with her. 'What's a car doing driving in here?' she whispered. 'This house isn't occupied.'

'How should I know?' her brother said impatiently. 'But I bet your bike's a mess.'

'I know,' she groaned, envisaging the twisted metal. 'Maybe——'

'Ssh!' she quietened him. 'Someone is getting out of the car.'

She watched as the man came around the back of the car, bending down to inspect what was left of her bicycle. He straightened, looking about him with narrowed grey eyes. He was a handsome man, although rather unkempt-looking, his hair long and out of style, although it gleamed with a clean black sheen, his eyes grey and piercing, his nose long and straight, his mouth set in a rigid line. He was very leanly built, although firmly muscled, his denims old and faded, the shirt he wore clean but unironed. He would be in his late thirties, Robyn guessed, his expression harsh, deep lines grooved into his face beside his nose and mouth.

She had been so mesmerised with the aggressively

male attractiveness of him that she had forgotten to hide, something she realised too late as he spotted her and strode angrily towards them.

'Now you've done it,' Billy glared at her.

'Shut up!' she snapped.

'Come out of there!' the man's angry voice ordered. 'Come on, I know you're in there,' he added at their delay.

'Now we're for it,' Billy muttered, dragging Robyn behind him as he stepped out into view.

Robyn looked up at the stranger, all six foot one of him, feeling like a midget herself at only five feet two inches. On closer inspection the man looked gaunt, very pale beneath his tan, the harshness to his features more noticeable.

'Well?' he barked as they remained silent. 'What have you to say for yourselves?'

'Sorry?' Billy said hopefully.

He received an impatient look for his trouble. 'I gather that distorted hunk of metal on the driveway belongs to one of you?'

'My sister,' Billy muttered, obviously realising this man was a force to be reckoned with.

Robyn's violet eyes flashed. 'It was a bicycle before you drove over it,' she snapped her indignation.

Glacial grey eyes were turned on her. 'I'm well aware of what it was. What I want to know is what it was doing on my driveway.'

She gasped. '*Your* driveway?'

'That's right.' He pushed the untidy dark hair back from his forehead as if it annoyed him.

'You live here?' Billy's eyes were as wide as saucers.

The man's mouth twisted. 'I do. Your names?' he rasped.

'William,' Billy supplied, obviously disconcerted by this man owning Orchard House, seeing his days of playing football here fast disappearing. 'Er—Billy, actually—sir.'

'And you?' Piercing grey eyes were now turned on Robyn.

'Robyn,' she supplied abruptly. After all, she had only come in here to help Billy. Although there were the condemning daffodils in her hand!

'Robyn . . .?' he prompted.

'Castle,' she muttered, feeling like a juvenile caught out in a misdemeanour, and not the eighteen-year-old she really was.

'You too?' he eyed Billy.

'Yes,' he muttered.

The man nodded. 'You have two minutes to get off my land,' he told them grimly. 'And take the bicycle with you.'

Robyn grimaced. 'I doubt it's worth the trouble.'

The man took out his wallet, taking out some notes. 'It's only the back wheel,' he held out the money towards her. 'This should replace it.'

She looked at him suspiciously. 'You're offering to pay for the damage?'

'As long as you're both gone in the allotted two minutes. And make sure any of your hooligan friends know not to come trespassing here again.'

'Hooligans . . .?' Robyn gasped.

'What else would you call yourselves?' he mocked, looking down at their identical clothing of denims and tight tee-shirts, although Robyn's were slightly more disreputable than Billy's.

She always dressed casually on Sundays, her job in the library calling for smartness at all times. 'You are in the eyes of the public,' Mr Leaven had told her on the one occasion she had dared to wear trousers. She had never dared again.

But Sundays were her own, and if she wanted to wear

her old denims and one of Billy's tee-shirts then surely
that was up to her. The fact that both items were now a
little the worse for wear was still nothing to do with this
arrogant man.

'You only have a minute left to take the money and
run,' the man drawled. 'I would advise you to do just
that.'

'I——'

'Yes, sir,' Billy interrupted her, taking the offered
money. 'Thank you, sir. Come on, Robyn. Robyn!' he
said pointedly when she looked like continuing the
argument.

She shook off his hand, reluctantly following him to
the driveway, unaware of the fact that the man had
followed them until he opened his car door in preparation of continuing on his way to the house.

'And make sure you remember what I said,' his voice
was harsh. 'I don't want you or any of your friends here
again.' He swung into the car, slamming the door after
him before driving off.

'He needn't worry, we won't be back,' Robyn
exploded. 'Rude man!' she added with disgust.

Billy burst out laughing at her indignant expression.
'He had a right to be annoyed.'

She looked down disgustedly at her bike. 'Just look
at this! It means I'll have to get the bus to work
tomorrow now,' she groaned; the bus service to this
sleepy little village was not very reliable at the best
of times. The bus company seemed to take buses out
of service without informing the people waiting for
them. Before she had taken to riding her bicycle the
three miles each way to Ampthull she had been late
for work many times simply because they had
decided not to run the bus she usually caught on that
particular day.

Billy helped her pull the bicycle up on its one straight

wheel and one bent one. 'Maybe he'll give you a lift in his Jag,' he teased.

She grimaced, putting the daffodils in the front basket. After all, he hadn't asked for them back! 'Is that what it is?' The type of car the man had been driving hadn't been of particular interest to her, what he had done with it had been.

'Mm,' her brother smiled appreciatively. 'Fantastic, wasn't it?'

Robyn looked down pointedly at her bicycle. 'I didn't notice. I'd better get this home and see if Dad thinks it can be salvaged.'

'I'll help you,' Billy offered instantly, lifting the damaged wheel off the ground while Robyn took control of the handlebars. 'Here's your money,' he handed it to her.

She took it and put it in her back pocket, not even bothering to count it. 'Why are you being so nice?' she asked suspiciously.

He gave her a look of feigned innocence, looking quite cherubic with his baby blond curls and fresh-scrubbed look. 'I'm always nice to you,' he grinned.

'Like hell you are——'

'I'll tell Mum you've been swearing,' he announced triumphantly, a look of satisfaction to his face.

'Oh, I see!' She had to smile, humour got the better of her. 'You don't want me to tell Mum and Dad about the game of football, right?'

'Right,' he admitted reluctantly. 'You won't, will you? Dad said he would stop my pocket-money for a month if I did it again.'

She raised her eyebrows questioningly. 'Then why did you?'

Billy sighed his impatience with her. 'Are you going to tell them or aren't you?'

She sighed. 'Of course I'm not.'

He immediately dropped the damaged end of her bicycle. 'See you later,' he grinned before running off.

'I didn't promise,' she called after him.

He turned round and poked his tongue out at her. 'I know you,' he scorned. 'You won't let me down.'

Little devil! The trouble was he knew she *wouldn't* let him down. She seemed to have spent the majority of her eighteen years getting Billy out of one scrape or another—and covering up for him. The five years' difference in their ages had made her protective towards him, over-protective on occasion, forging a bond between them that meant she would always stand by him, no matter what he did.

It took her twice as long as it should have done to get home, mainly because of Billy's defection, and it was with some relief that she leant her bicycle up against the garden shed before going into the house.

'I'll have a look at it later,' her father assured her when she explained that it was damaged. 'Did you happen to see Billy while you were out?'

She hastily looked away. 'I think I might have done, I'm not too sure.'

Her father gave her a reproving look, not fooled by her evasion for one moment. 'He'll be home for lunch, I presume,' he said dryly, one eyebrow arched enquiringly.

'Oh yes—Yes, I suppose so. He usually is, isn't he?' She bit her lip at her slip-up, seeing her father's amused smile and smiling back at him.

Her father owned the local shop and post office, her mother actually running the shop part of it, her father running the post office and delivering groceries to the people in the village who found it difficult getting down to the shop, mainly the older members of the community. It was a good arrangement, the shop was very profitable, and even Robyn occasionally helped out on her days off from the library when they were particularly busy.

'What's actually wrong with your bike?' her father frowned now, sitting back comfortably in his chair, puffing away contentedly on his pipe, the newspaper open in his hand, enjoying the luxury of his one day off.

Robyn looked uncomfortable. 'The back wheel's a bit bent,' she told him lamely.

'How bent?'

'Very,' she admitted with a grimace.

He put the newspaper down. 'How did that happen?'

'A slight accident,' she revealed reluctantly.

'Accident?' her mother repeated sharply as she bustled into the room with the vase of daffodils. 'You haven't had an accident, have you, Robyn?' She looked anxiously at her daughter's slender body.

Robyn and Billy both took after their father with their fair colouring and lean frames; their mother was short and dark, her figure on the portly side. She loved village life, enjoyed running the shop, although she enjoyed looking after her family most of all; her cooking was out of this world. Robyn often teased her mother about the fact that she only had to look at one of her own delicious cakes to put on pounds, whereas the rest of them could eat any number of them and not put on an ounce.

'Not me, Mum,' she grinned at her. 'My bike. It— er—It sort of got driven over,' she told them ruefully.

'Were you on it?' her father asked concernedly.

'No,' she laughed. 'I was—I was picking those flowers for Mum,' she explained, omitting the fact that they had been growing in the garden of Orchard House when she picked them. 'My bike was on the side of the road and the car drove straight over it.'

'Did it stop?'

'Oh yes,' she answered her mother. 'Did you know that someone was living in Orchard House?'

Her mother nodded. 'Mr Howarth. He's been there two or three weeks now. Was he the one who drove over your bicycle?'

'Yes, but it was my fault. I shouldn't have left it outside his home. I was in the woods on the other side of the road picking those wild daffodils for you when it happened,' she invented. 'Mr Howarth?' she questioned curiously, wondering why her mother hadn't mentioned him before.

'Richard Howarth—Rick, I think he said.' Her mother rearranged the flowers in the vase. 'He's had the odd piece of grocery from the shop. I think he must do his main food shopping in Ampthull, because he's only ever had the occasional loaf of bread and a few jars of coffee.'

'Actually I don't think he does shop in Ampthull,' Robyn said slowly. 'I don't think he shops anywhere.'

'You mean he doesn't eat?' Her mother was scandalised, believing that food was the panacea for all ills.

She shook her head. 'Not so that you would notice.' She frowned. 'It was really strange—by his clothes he looked down and out, really unkempt, and yet he was driving a Jaguar, this year's model too. You don't suppose he stole it, do you?' she asked eagerly, sensing a mystery.

'Don't be silly, Robyn,' her mother said sternly. 'Mr Howarth seems to be a highly educated man. Maybe he's just an eccentric.'

'Maybe.' But she didn't think so. Rick Howarth hadn't liked them on his land, had wanted to protect his privacy at all costs. He looked and dressed like a tramp, and yet he drove a very expensive car, and as her mother had said, he spoke in a highly educated voice. Perhaps her mother was right after all, maybe he was an eccentric.

Her mother frowned now. 'I don't like to think of him not eating.'

Her husband put down his newspaper. 'How about the fact that I'm not eating?' he grinned at her. 'Isn't lunch ready yet?'

'You're always thinking of your stomach!'

Robyn chuckled as her mother flounced out of the room to serve the lunch. 'It would serve you right if Mum didn't give you any,' she told her father.

He laughed. 'She wouldn't be that cruel!'

No, she wouldn't. Her parents had a very happy marriage; they were ideally suited in every way, and their business partnership was as successful as their personal one.

The bus service was erratic as usual the next day, and Robyn arrived ten minutes late at the library, earning a disapproving look from Mr Leaven.

She loved working in the library, had a passion for books that bordered on obsession. Just to touch a book to anticipate devouring its pages, filled her with a warm pleasure. Which was the reason Mr Leaven hardly ever gave her the job of tidying the fiction shelves. She would become lost to her surroundings, engrossed in a newly discovered book, and the other books on the shelves would remain in disarray.

Consequently she was quite surprised when Mr Leaven told her to tidy the books back into order, although she quickly made her escape before he changed his mind.

She wasn't quite as happy when she saw who she was to be working with. Selma! No wonder she had been sent to work with her; everyone else had probably opted out. Not that Selma wasn't friendly—she was, too friendly upon occasion. She thought nothing of recounting all the intimate details of her life to anyone who happened to be around at the time. The trouble

was that she demanded equally intimate revelations in
return.

There was no opportunity today to linger over a newly
discovered book, listening half-heartedly as Selma chat-
tered on about the fantastic new boy she had met over
the weekend, becoming more friendly with him in those
two days than Robyn intended becoming with any man
before she married him!

'What about you?' Selma stopped in the H section,
well out of Mr Leaven's view.

Robyn blinked her puzzlement. 'What about me?'

'Do you have a boy-friend, silly?' Selma giggled.

Robyn blushed. When around Selma, a girl very
popular with the opposite sex, she felt more than a little
embarrassed about her own boy-friendless state.

'You mean you don't?' Selma saw that blush and
interpreted it correctly.

Irritation flashed in her violet-blue eyes. 'I didn't say
that,' she snapped.

Selma looked interested. 'So you do have a boy-
friend?'

'I—Yes. Yes, I have a boy-friend.' Now why had she
said that, why lie about something that wasn't after all
important?

'What's his name?'

'His name?' Robyn repeated slowly, licking her lips
to delay answering. 'It's—er—it's Richard,' she said in
a rush. 'Rick, actually—Rick Howarth.' God, this was
getting worse, the lie was becoming deeper and deeper.
It was just that she couldn't stand Selma's derision.

The other girl always had at least one man in tow,
whereas Robyn had only ever had the odd date, and
very rarely with the same boy twice. She wasn't interested in football or cars, and as that seemed to be all
her dates ever wanted to talk about she usually ended
up by not saying a word all evening. It had earned her

the reputation of being 'stuck-up', an erroneous impression, but one that seemed to have lasted. Consequently she very rarely dated, something Selma had probably heard about.

She certainly had all of the other girl's attention now. 'Where did you meet him?' Selma wanted to know.

'He—He's just moved into Sanford,' at least this part was true! 'I met him at the weekend.'

'Is he nice?' Selma asked eagerly.

'Very.'

'Good-looking?'

Robyn nodded. 'Yes.'

The other girl frowned. 'Don't you want to talk about him?'

Robyn concentrated on her work with an intensity she was far from feeling. 'Not particularly,' she replied in a bored voice.

'Keeping him to yourself, are you?' Selma teased, not at all offended by Robyn's attitude.

'Something like that,' she nodded, wishing this conversation over.

'When are you seeing him again?'

'I—er—Tonight, probably,' she invented, wishing she had never started this.

'Going anywhere nice?' Selma wanted to know.

'I'm not sure. Probably just to his house.' Robyn wished she could move away, put an end to these lies, and yet she knew that this job usually took most of the morning to complete. If Selma was going to ask her questions about Richard Howarth all that time . . .! She was going to run out of conversation about him any moment now!

Selma's eyes widened. 'You've met his parents?'

She shook her head. 'He has his own house.'

'He does?' That took the other girl aback.

'Yes.' She moved on to the I section, getting nearer

and nearer Mr Leaven's desk, and she hoped nearer to ending this discussion.

Selma looked wistful. 'I've never been out with a boy who had his own house. I usually have to wait until his parents go out.'

Wait for what? Robyn almost asked. Selma was a pretty girl, black hair kept long past her shoulders, deep brown eyes, a clear complexion, a nice slim figure, and yet she had earnt herself rather a bad reputation with the boys in the area. Most of them were willing to go out with her for a while, but they all ended up marrying someone else. It was a shame really, because she was a very nice girl given the chance to be.

'He must be quite rich to own his own house,' she remarked now.

'I have no idea.' Robyn moved up to the J section, luckily almost in view of Mr Leaven.

'Or does he just rent it?' He had obviously stepped down in Selma's estimation if he did.

'I——'

'Would you two girls kindly get on with your work—quietly.' Mr Leaven suddenly appeared behind them. 'It may have escaped your notice,' he continued in an angry whisper, 'but this is supposed to be a library, a place where people can come to quietly read and study. Your voices——'

'Ssh!' A woman at a nearby table looked up to glare at him. 'Can't you read?' she hissed, pointing to the sigh that read 'QUIET, PLEASE, PEOPLE WORKING'.

'Get on with your work!' Mr Leaven snapped at Robyn and Selma before returning to his desk.

'Oh dear,' Selma giggled. 'That's put him in a bad mood for the rest of the day!'

Indeed it had, and Robyn kept out of his way as much as possible. She kept out of Selma's way too, not being anxious to reopen the subject of Rick Howarth. She felt slightly ashamed of herself for using him in that way, even if he didn't know about it. She had thought it would get Selma off the subject of her having a boy-friend, and instead she seemed to have made matters worse. She hoped she would have forgotten all about it by tomorrow.

The bus service was dreadful again that night, and the shop was already closed and her mother in the kitchen when she entered the house. 'The bus,' came her moody explanation for her lateness.

Her mother nodded. 'I thought you might be late, so I made a casserole for dinner.'

'Lovely!' Robyn ran upstairs to change into her denims and tee-shirt, the rumblings of her stomach making it a hurried change. She was always ravenously hungry in the evenings, and so was Billy. Her brother didn't utter a word as he ate his portion of the chicken casserole.

'I mended your bike today, Robyn,' her father told her, eating his meal at a more leisurely pace.

'You did?' Her eyes lit up with gratitude, as she thought of not having to catch the bus again tomorrow.

'Mm. I took one of the wheels off your mother's old bike. She never rides it anyway.'

'So you didn't need to buy a new wheel?' she frowned.

'No,' he shook his head.

'That means you'll have to give the money back,' Billy emerged from eating his dessert long enough to utter.

'Money?' their mother repeated sharply. 'What money is this, Robyn?'

She refused dessert, although she knew the apple pie would be delicious—her mother's cooking always was. 'Mr Howarth gave me some money yesterday when he drove over my bicycle. I'd forgotten all about it.' She reached into the back pocket of her denims, taking out the notes she had stuffed there yesterday.

'Wow!' Billy breathed slowly, looking at the two crumpled ten-pound notes Robyn held in her hand.

'Wow, indeed.' Their father looked disapprovingly over the top of his glasses. 'You had no right accepting money from Mr Howarth, not when you openly admitted it was your fault for leaving your bike on the road.'

Robyn was still dazed herself by the amount of money Rick Howarth had given her. Her bike was only an old one, more or less ready for the scrap-merchant who came round every couple of months—the whole thing wasn't worth twenty pounds! 'I'll give it back,' she said hurriedly.

'You most certainly will,' her father said firmly. 'And as for you, young man,' he turned towards Billy, 'how did you know Mr Howarth gave Robyn some money?'

'I—er—I——'

'I told him,' Robyn instantly defended. 'Last night.'

'Yes, that's right,' Billy agreed eagerly. 'Last night when we were playing Monopoly.'

'Mm,' their father looked sceptical. 'Well, you can return that money as soon as possible,' he told Robyn.

'Tonight,' her mother put in firmly, standing up. 'I have an extra casserole and an apple pie to go over to Mr Howarth. I was going to get Billy to take it over, but you might as well take it, Robyn, as you're going anyway.'

Robyn stood up to help clear the table. 'Do I have to, Mum? I don't mind taking the money back, but do I have to take the food too? Besides, it's my night to do the washing-up.'

'Billy can do it. Oh yes, you can,' his mother insisted as he went to protest. 'Your father has had a hard day.'

'But I was going to football practice,' Billy moaned.

'This will only take you five minutes, you can go to your football practice afterwards.'

'But——'

'Billy!'

'Yes, Dad.' He dutifully went into the kitchen, knowing when their father used that tone that he would brook no argument.

Robyn knew that there was no point in her arguing either. She was going to have to take that casserole and pie over to Orchard House whether she wanted to or not. And she didn't want to. Spending a couple of minutes giving Rick Howarth back his money was one thing, delivering a food parcel was another. If only she hadn't told her mother that she didn't think he was eating! She had put herself in this predicament by a few thoughtless words. And what Rick Howarth would make of her bringing him food she wouldn't like to guess!

'I don't know why you're so miserable,' Billy muttered as he wiped up. 'At least you got out of this!' He pulled a face.

'Shame!' she said unsympathetically, packing the food into a tin so that she could carry it more easily. 'Just think yourself lucky you don't have to go and face the ogre. After yesterday I don't fancy seeing him again.'

'What was that?' her mother asked as she bustled out of the larder with a jar of her homemade marmalade.

'Nothing, Mum,' Robyn answered hastily. 'Has that got to go too?' she indicated the jar.

'Yes. I thought of sending jam, but not everyone likes jam. But I know he likes marmalade, he bought a jar when he first moved in. Now can you manage all that?'

Robyn balanced the jar on top of the tin. 'I think so. If you could just open the door for me?'

The tin weighed heavy in her arms, and despite her reluctance to reach Orchard House she found herself hurrying down the road, anxious to get rid of her heavy burden.

Orchard House looked unlived-in and neglected, and if it weren't for the Jaguar parked outside and the thin spiral of smoke coming from the chimney she would have said the place was empty. There were no curtains at the windows, no sign of movement within.

Her knock on the front door received no reply, so she went around the back and tried there. Still no answer. But he had to be there, he would hardly go out and leave a lit fire. Besides, there was the Jaguar, his transport.

She knocked again, and still receiving no answer she tentatively turned the doorhandle and walked in. There were a couple of used mugs in the sink, but other than that the kitchen was bare, the cooker looked unused, the cupboards apparently empty. Surely no one could actually live in such discomfort?

Which brought her back to the whereabouts of Rick Howarth. He obviously spent little time in the kitchen, so leaving the tin and the jar of marmalade on the kitchen table she decided to search the rest of the house. Each room proved to be empty of furniture and habitation, having a musty smell to it. The last bedroom she came to seemed to be the one with the fire in, although the room still struck chill. There was a single bed, a table containing a typewriter, one hard-looking chair, and no other furniture.

Robyn repressed a shiver as she went back downstairs. How could anyone live in such starkness of human comfort? That brought back the question of why Rick Howarth was living in such conditions. Could her first assumption be correct, could he be a thief on the run?

And yet a village certainly wasn't the best place to use as a hideout, a town was much better for obscurity, and Rick Howarth appeared to her to be intelligent enough to realise that. In a village the size of Sanford you couldn't even sneeze without the neighbours knowing about it, and a newcomer aroused much attention;

her own mother's interest in Rick Howarth was evidence
of that. Her mother wasn't a nosey person, and yet even
she seemed to have learnt a little about the new occupier
of Orchard House.

But where was he? The house was empty, and yet he
didn't appear to be the type who enjoyed gardening.
Did he look *any* type?

She returned to the kitchen, in a quandary about what
to do. She couldn't just leave the food here, he would
wonder where it came from, and if she took the food
back home her mother would want to know why. But
she could have to wait ages for him to come back, she
had no way of knowing——

'What the hell are you doing in here?'

Robyn swung round, paling as she saw Rick Howarth
standing dark and dangerous in the doorway.

CHAPTER TWO

THE jar of marmalade she had been toying with slipped out of her hand and smashed on the tiled floor with a resounding crash, and she groaned as the sticky contents began to spread all over the floor. 'Do you have a cloth?' she asked desperately, going down on her hands and knees to begin picking up the bigger pieces of glass.

'What the hell——!' Strong sinewy fingers came out and Rick Howarth grasped her arm roughly, pulling her effortlessly to her feet. 'Are you stupid, girl?' he rasped, looking down at her contemptuously as she struggled to be free.

Her head went back, her eyes flashing deeply violet in her anger. 'Of course I'm not stupid, Mr Howarth,' she snapped. 'You just startled me, and I——I dropped the marmalade.'

'I can see that.' His mouth twisted.

'Then you can also see that the floor is in a mess,' she scorned.

He gave an impatient sigh before moving to the cupboard under the sink unit, taking out some ragged pieces of material and throwing them down on the table in front of her. 'Here,' he said abruptly, 'help yourself.'

'Thanks,' she muttered, getting down on to the floor once again to wipe up the broken glass. It really was a mess——glass among the sticky concoction that was all that was left of her mother's beautiful home-made marmalade.

'I'm still waiting to find out what you're doing in my home,' he said tersely, his face a harsh mask, deep lines grooved beside his mouth.

He was no better dressed than he had been yesterday, the denims and shirt were still as disreputable, although the over-long dark hair looked newly washed, slightly waving as it grew low down over his collar.

'I did knock,' she told him resentfully. 'And when there was no answer——'

'You just walked in,' he finished coldly.

'No!' Robyn defended indignantly. 'Well—yes. But it wasn't quite like that!'

'It never is.' Rick Howarth's mouth twisted contemptuously.

Colour flooded her cheeks at his rude manner. 'I didn't come here to be insulted——'

'If you didn't violate people's privacy perhaps you wouldn't be,' he snapped angrily, his eyes cold. 'This is the second time in as many days that I've caught you on my property uninvited. Well?' he quirked an eyebrow mockingly. 'No comeback?'

Robyn bit her lip. 'No,' she admitted reluctantly, knowing she couldn't deny the truth. 'But——'

'Don't go into lengthy explanations,' he said dismissively, obviously bored by the subject—as he was probably bored with her! 'Sufficient to say you were trespassing, the reasons don't really matter. And today you're doing it again, although you have some nerve actually entering the house.'

'I told you, I——'

'You knocked and there was no answer,' he scorned. 'When that happens it's the usual practice to go away and come back some other time.'

Robyn stood up at last, dropping the glass and sticky rags into the bin in the corner of the room. It was still sticky on the floor, but if Rick Howarth wanted it any cleaner he could damn well do it himself.

'I was going away,' she snapped. 'I *am* going away, and I don't intend coming back again—ever!' She moved

to the table, taking the lid off the tin. 'I'll just leave
these with you,' she slammed the dishes down on the
table. 'If you could return the crockery when you've
finished with it I'm sure my mother would be grateful.'
She made a great clatter, deliberately so, as she put the
lid back on the tin, just wanting to get away from this
rude, ungrateful pig of a man.

He came over to look at the casserole and the pie.
'What's this?' he rasped, his eyes narrowed.

Heavens, anyone would think they were trying to
poison him! 'What does it look like?' she derided, sighing
at his blank expression. 'It's food, Mr Howarth.
Chicken,' she indicated the deepest dish. 'Apple,' she
pointed to the other one.

'What's it doing here?'

'My mother thought you were in need of sustenance.'
She gave the impression that she personally couldn't give
a damn if he expired of starvation in front of her eyes.

His mouth tightened, his eyes glacial. 'Your mother?'

'Mrs Castle. She runs the village shop,' Robyn explained with sarcastic patience.

'Ah yes, I remember her,' he nodded, his gaze shar-
pening. 'And who gave her the impression that I looked
in need of being fed?'

Once again colour stained her cheeks. 'Well—I——'

'You did,' he accused. 'Well, I don't need any hand-
outs, Miss Castle,' he told her furiously, his eyes glitter-
ing dangerously. 'So you can tell your mother——'

'No, Mr Howarth, *you* can tell her, when you return
the dishes.' She walked to the door, two bright spots of
angry colour in her cheeks. 'I'm certainly got going to
tell her what an ungrateful swine you are!' and she flung
open the door.

'Just a minute,' he ground out, grasping her arm in
exactly the same place as before, adding further bruises
she was sure. 'Don't be in such a hurry to leave.'

'But you said——'

'I didn't ask you to leave.'

'You were rude about my mother,' she flared. 'She was only trying to be friendly, and you threw her gesture back in her face.'

'Okay, okay.' He let go of her arm, running a hand round the back of his neck in a weary gesture, looking down helplessly at the casserole. 'Maybe I was a little ungrateful.'

'A little?' she scoffed.

'Okay, I was rude,' he accepted with a sigh.

'You were, very.'

His mouth twisted into the semblance of a smile, the first lessening of his harshness that she had seen. 'Don't go over the top, Miss Castle,' he drawled. 'Just tell me what I have to do with this,' he indicated the casserole, 'to be able to eat it.'

Robyn frowned. 'You heat it up.'

'How?' he asked helplessly.

She searched his hard face for any sign of mockery, but could see none. 'You really don't know how?'

'I would hardly be asking if I did,' he derided.

'But I—You—Surely you must have been eating *something* in the time you've been here?' She was incredulous at the thought of him not eating at all, although the whipcord leanness of him didn't seem to indicate that he had been over-indulging.

He shrugged his broad shoulders. 'The odd sandwich. And apples.' He held up the apples he had brought in with him. 'My dinner—I ran out of bread this morning.'

Robyn shook her head. 'That's ridiculous! What are you trying to do, kill yourself?'

Rick Howarth's face darkened. 'Mind your own damned business, Miss Castle,' he rasped angrily, his features once again hard. 'My eating habits are none of your concern.'

'My comment wasn't meant literally,' she told him coldly, her head held high in challenge. 'Although you don't look well,' she added daringly, waiting for the explosion.

It didn't come; his face was suddenly pale. 'I don't feel well,' he admitted shakily, swaying slightly on his feet.

Robyn rushed to his side, her arm going supportively about his waist. Although if he did pass out she would never be able to hold him up! 'Sit down,' she instructed firmly, envisaging an argument and not getting one as he pulled out one of the kitchen chairs and sat down. 'When did you last eat?' she asked concernedly.

'I told you, I had the last of the bread this morning.'

She really didn't like the look of him, he was very pale. 'How much?' she probed.

He shrugged. 'One slice, I think.'

'And before that?'

'I had some apples yesterday,' he said after a moment's thought.

Robyn sighed. 'No wonder you're feeling weak! I'll heat up the casserole for you if you'll just sit there.'

His mouth twisted. 'I wasn't thinking of going anywhere.'

She was conscious of him watching her as she moved about the kitchen, miraculously finding a saucepan, a plate and some cutlery. The cooker was a very old model, probably left here by old Mrs Bird who had last lived here. But at least the cooker worked, that was something.

She turned round to find Rick Howarth still watching her, obviously completely recovered from the weakness that had suddenly washed over him. 'Will you stop staring at me?' she said irritably, muttering to herself as she burnt her finger on the rim of the saucepan. 'Now look what you've made me do,' she accused crossly, backing away as he stood up to come towards her, very dark and overwhelming in the close confines of this small room.

'Let me see.' He held out his hand for hers.

She shook her head. 'It's nothing.'

'I want to see,' he repeated firmly.

Robyn thrust her hand at him, gritting her teeth as he took his time inspecting it. She surreptitiously watched him beneath lowered lashes. He really was a very handsome individual, so much so that it gave her the butterflies just to be near him. But there was a mystery about him, one that made her feel nervous of being alone with him like this. After all, she didn't know the first thing about him.

His mouth twisted derisively. 'Just a superficial burn.' He dropped her hand, his touch having been gentle but firm.

'I could have told you that!' She turned back to the cooker, her emotions disturbed as she served the casserole on to a plate before putting it down on the table.

'Thanks.' He sat down and began eating, slowly at first, and then with increasing appetite. 'This is very good,' he looked up long enough to say appreciatively.

'I'm sure my mother will be glad to hear that,' Robyn snapped sarcastically.

He sighed. 'Look, I've apologised——'

'No, you haven't,' she instantly contradicted, placing black unsugared coffee in front of him, having found an old tin kettle that she had boiled the water up in on the top of the cooker, but unable to find milk or sugar. The store-cupboard contained only coffee, the refrigerator was completely empty.

'Maybe I haven't,' he accepted grudgingly. 'But precocious kids——'

'Kid!' she cut in indignantly, her eyes blazing.

Rick Howarth smiled at her reaction, looking a lot less grim now that he had eaten something. 'All right, schoolchildren of an indiscriminate age——'

She drew an angry breath. 'I'm not a schoolgirl, Mr Howarth. I'm eighteen.'

His gaze ran insolently over her slender body. 'You aren't very filled out for an eighteen-year-old.'

'And you're the scruffiest individual I've ever seen,' she told him furiously, angered by his outspoken insults. She might not be voluptuous, but she had all the right curves in the right places—even if he was blind to them.

'I am, aren't I?' he agreed with casual acceptance.

'Yes!' she snapped. 'And your hair needs cutting too.'

He sat back, his plate empty. 'What are you like as a barber?'

Her eyes widened to large violet orbs. 'I'm not offering to cut your hair for you!'

'I'm asking.'

'But I—I don't even know you!'

His smile was mocking. 'Do you have to know someone before you can cut their hair?'

She was near exploding point at his audacity. 'I came over here to return your money—Oh goodness,' she groaned, 'I haven't given it to you.' She took it out of her pocket and put it on the table. 'I didn't need it after all,' she explained. 'Besides, this was much too much.'

He made no effort to pick up the money, almost as if it meant nothing to him. 'How come you didn't use it?'

'Dad took one off another bike we had. Anyway, as I was saying, I only came here to return that money and deliver the food——'

'Talking of food——' he eyed the apple pie she had just taken from the oven.

'Help yourself,' she slammed the dish down on the table. 'I didn't come here to act as your cook or to cut your hair!'

'Your mother really is a very good cook.' He quirked one dark eyebrow. 'I don't suppose you can cook as well?'

Robyn flushed. 'Not as well, no. Why, were you thinking of offering me a job as your housekeeper?' she scorned.

'That's not a bad idea.'

'It's a lousy idea. Look, I have to go now. I've been here far too long already.' Her parents would wonder what on earth she was doing over here all this time.

'What about my hair?' he drawled.

'Go to a professional barber,' Robyn advised impatiently. 'I have to get home now, it's starting to get dark.'

Rick Howarth stood up, looking infinitely more relaxed than when she had first arrived. 'I'll drive you,' he offered.

'There's no need. It isn't far,' she babbled. 'I can quite easily walk.'

'I said I'll drive you. I wouldn't like you to get attacked on the way.'

'In Sanford?' she derided.

'Anywhere,' he said seriously. 'There are woods on the way back to your home, you could be dragged in there and no one would be any the wiser.'

'Thanks!' her mouth twisted derisively. 'If I felt all right about it before I certainly don't now!'

He opened the door for her. 'Okay, let's go.' He moved to unlock the car door.

'Shouldn't you lock up the house?' she asked once they were seated in the car.

He eyes her with some amusement. 'There's nothing in there for anyone to take.' He manoeuvred the car out of the driveway into the road.

Robyn frowned. 'Why don't you have any furniture?'

His mouth tightened. 'How do you know I don't?' he asked suspiciously.

She swallowed hard, realising her mistake too late.
'I—er—I——'

'So you went prying around my home,' he said
harshly, his face rigid with anger. 'I should have known,
I suppose. All women are the same, aren't they, you just
can't leave a man's privacy alone.'

Robyn gasped at his accusations. 'I only looked——'

'Because you were damned nosey,' he rasped.

'No——'

'Yes!' His teeth snapped together angrily.

'Please, Mr Howarth——'

He drew the car to a halt. 'This is your home, isn't
it?' he said coldly, staring straight ahead of him.

She looked about them in a daze the short drive to her
home seemed to have taken no time at all. 'I—Yes.
But——'

'Goodnight, Miss Castle. Thank your mother for
me.'

'I—Yes, yes I will.' She scrambled out of the car. 'I
just wish you would let me explain.'

'There's nothing to explain.' He accelerated the
Jaguar forward with a screech of the tyres, the passenger door slamming closed with the force of the
speed.

Whew! What a volatile man—one minute almost
human, the next back to the cold hard stranger she had
first encountered. Admittedly she had no right to be
walking around his home, but if she hadn't been worried
as to his whereabouts she wouldn't have done such a
thing.

'You've been gone a long time, dear.' Her mother
looked up from her knitting as Robyn entered the
lounge. 'Have you been round to Kay's?'

How she would have liked to have used her friend as
an excuse, to have avoided all the curious questions that
were bound to be asked once her family learnt she had

been with Rick Howarth for the last hour and a half. But she couldn't deliberately lie.

She sat down in one of the armchairs. 'Mr Howarth wasn't feeling too well——'

'Oh dear,' her mother frowned. 'He isn't ill, is he?'

'No, it was just lack of food.'

'Did he eat what I sent him?'

'Yes, that's why I was so long. I—I wanted to make sure he ate it.'

'Very wise,' her mother nodded thoughtfully. 'I don't like to see a man starve himself for any reason.'

Somehow Robyn didn't think Rick Howarth was in the habit of going without his food. But she didn't think he was in the habit of getting it himself either! He had been totally lost in the kitchen, and she would swear that he hadn't used the cooker once in the three weeks he had been in residence. He was obviously used to someone getting his food for him, which pointed to him having a woman somewhere in the background of his life. Or he *had* would be more appropriate, because he was very much alone now. Maybe his marriage had broken up—a man of his age was sure to be married, which would account for his bitterness towards women.

'Well, at least he has a hot meal inside him now,' she told her mother. 'He said to thank you, and that you're a very good cook.'

Her mother flushed her pleasure. It wasn't often she received compliments on her cooking; her family all took such a luxury for granted, although they soon complained if there was anything wrong with it.

'I think he should get himself a housekeeper,' her mother said absently.

Robyn didn't tell her that Rick Howarth had half-heartedly offered her such a position. 'There isn't anything to "keep" in that house.' She bit her lip, realising she was being indiscreet. Rick Howarth certainly wouldn't thank her for discussing him in this way.

Her father peered over the top of his newspaper. 'What do you mean by that?' he asked in a puzzled voice.

She shrugged. 'He doesn't have a lot of furniture, that's all. But as he's alone I don't suppose he needs it.' She stood up. 'I think I'll go and wash my hair.' She hurriedly left the room, reluctant to talk about Rick Howarth any more.

Unfortunately everyone else seemed to want to know about him. 'Did you see your boy-friend last night?' Selma wanted to know the next day.

Robyn gave an inward groan, wishing she had never mentioned Rick Howarth to the other girl. 'He isn't my boy-friend,' she told Selma irritably.

'But you said he was.'

'Well, he—he's just a friend. And he happens to be male. That's really all there is to it.'

Selma shrugged. 'It's okay by me if you don't want to talk about him.'

'I didn't say that,' Robyn sighed. 'There's just nothing to tell.'

'Like I said, if you don't want to talk about him——'

'There's really nothing to tell,' Robyn repeated sharply.

Selma gave her a knowing glance. 'Had an argument, did you?'

'No!' she flashed, then realised that here was a way out of this. 'Yes,' she deliberately contradicted herself. 'We did, actually.'

'I shouldn't worry about it,' Selma shrugged. 'If he's really interested he'll be back.'

Considering the fact that Selma and the boy she had met over the weekend had already finished Robyn was surprised that the other girl felt qualified to offer this advice.

And Rick Howarth wouldn't be 'back' in her life at all, in fact she wouldn't be too upset if she never saw him again.

Her bicycle was back in use, so she wasn't late back home that evening, although the house was deserted when she went in. It was half day closing at the shop, so her parents should have been here. She found them out in the yard, her father covered in oil from where he was working under the van, her mother looking on anxiously.

'What's happened?' Robyn whispered to her mother, knowing that her father wouldn't welcome such a question. Having to do any sort of mechanical work on the van was guaranteed to put her father in a bad mood.

Her mother grimaced. 'It broke down on the delivery this afternoon. Your father had to get Mr Jeffs to help him push it back here.'

'Oh dear!' She could imagine her father's fury. 'Has he been working on it long?'

'About two hours,' her mother told her softly. 'Your dinner is in the oven. Your father and I will eat later.'

'Where's Billy?'

'Out delivering the groceries for us on his bike.'

Her eyes widened. 'The van broke down on the way *to* deliver the groceries?'

'Mm,' her mother nodded. 'Billy's been out delivering since he got home from school.'

Robyn's father appeared from under the van, his face smeared with oil. 'Hello, love,' he muttered. 'Pass me that spanner, Barbara. The one at your feet,' he added tersely as she hesitated.

'I think I'll go in and have my dinner,' Robyn whispered to her mother.

She smiled understandingly. 'I should.'

'Barbara, the spanner!'

'All right, Peter,' she said patiently, handing it to him.

'I'll be in in a moment,' she told Robyn.

Her mother's steak and kidney pie melted in the mouth; it was a favourite with Robyn. Her mother came in as she was washing up her used crockery.

'Everything all right?' Robyn asked.

She smiled. 'I think your father is just about finished. Billy's just got home too, so I think we might be able to have our meal now.'

Robyn frowned. 'There's still one box of groceries here.'

'Oh yes, that's Mr Howarth's.'

'Mr Howarth's . . .?' she echoed in dismay.

'Mm.' Her mother heated up the gravy. 'Billy didn't think you would mind taking that one over.'

'Well, I do! I don't want to go over there, Mum,' she said pleadingly. 'I—I didn't like him very much.'

'Don't be silly, dear, he's very nice. He came over with these today,' she indicated the carnations in the vase in the window. 'Besides, Billy has to get his homework done now. And it won't take you five minutes.'

'Oh, all right,' Robyn agreed grudgingly. 'Just give me a few minutes to change.'

She checked the contents of the box on the way over to Orchard House, finding quite a few easily prepared meals. Well, at least he was going to start eating now. Her mother had also put in an individual steak and kidney pie. Robyn shook her head; her mother was never happy unless she was trying to fatten someone up.

Rick Howarth answered her knock today. 'Well, well, well,' he drawled mockingly. 'If it isn't Little Miss Castle!'

She gave him an impatient glare. 'I brought your groceries.'

'I'd given up on them,' he held up the apple he had been eating.

'Here you are,' she held out the box towards him.

'My father had a little trouble with his delivery van.'

He made no effort to take the box from her, opening the kitchen door wider for her to enter, which she did, reluctantly, shooting him a suspicious glance as he closed the door behind her.

'I'm not staying,' she told him stiffly, once again unnerved by him.

His eyes were narrowed to grey slits. 'Why aren't you?'

'I wouldn't want to be accused of snooping again.'

His mouth twisted. 'So you hold grudges, do you?'

'Certainly not!' Her eyes flashed her indignation. 'I just didn't think you liked company.'

'I don't,' he acknowledged abruptly. 'Or at least, I didn't.'

Her eyes widened, some of her resentment leaving her. 'Are you saying you don't mind my being here?'

'Exactly.' He threw the half eaten apple in the bin, holding up the steak and kidney pie. 'What do I do with this?'

Robyn took it out of his hand, flicking the switch on the cooker and putting the pie inside. 'I know what I'd like to do with it,' she said vehemently. 'And it isn't anything pleasant.'

'I didn't think it would be,' Rick Howarth said dryly.

'Well, I can't believe you're so helpless.' She peeled a couple of potatoes from the box and put them on to cook. 'You look so—so—well, capable,' she finished lamely.

'Oh, I am,' he leant back against the sink unit, 'at some things. Cooking isn't one of them.'

'Neither is ironing, by the look of you,' she grimaced at his clean but creased shirt.

He looked down at it too. 'They turn out this way from the launderette.'

'That's because they should be ironed afterwards,' she

sighed. 'They look expensive shirts too.'

'Do they?' his tone was distant. 'It never occurred to me.'

Once again he had clammed up when she had got too personal. 'Well, they do,' she persisted stubbornly, wondering at her own nerve. This man had shown her more than once that he didn't like any sort of interference from her, any reference of a personal nature. 'You should iron them before wearing them,' she added.

'Are these ready yet?' He lifted up the lid of the saucepan to look at the potatoes.

'No!' She angrily replaced the lid. 'What on earth do you do here all day on your own?' she asked with exasperation.

His expression became remote, his eyes cold. 'This and that,' he evaded tautly.

Robyn sighed. 'Why are you so secretive?'

'Why are you so nosey?' he rasped.

She drew in a ragged breath, looking very young and vulnerable in a fitted light blue tee-shirt—one that definitely showed her curves!—and a navy blue and white cotton-print skirt, her short blonde hair newly washed, her face bare of make-up.

Rick Howarth was obviously aware of her youth too, his eyes narrowing ominously. 'I must be insane,' he muttered. 'Or desperate,' he added disgustedly.

'Why?' she asked in a puzzled voice, realising his mood had changed yet again. He certainly was a moody person!

'Wasting my time talking to an eighteen-year-old,' he answered bluntly.

Robyn gasped, paling at his intended insult, her hands shaking as she clenched them at her side. 'You're not only rude,' she quavered, 'you're deliberately hurtful too!' She ran to the door, intending to make her escape before she made a fool of herself.

'Robyn——'

She swung round, her bottom lip trembling precariously. 'It's all right, Mr Howarth,' she choked, her look defiant. 'I'll leave and save you the trouble of wasting any more time.'

'Robyn . . .' He shook his head. 'I didn't mean it the way it sounded. I'm thirty-six. Do you know what that means?'

'That you're old!' she retorted childishly.

His mouth quirked with humour. 'I think I deserved that. Being thirty-six doesn't necessarily mean I'm too old, it just means you're too young.'

She frowned. 'For what?'

He sighed his exasperation. 'For—for this!' His head lowered and he caught up her lips with his, moving them slowly against her in a slow, drugging kiss.

It was so unexpected that Robyn just froze, accepting the kiss although not exactly responding to it. She had been kissed in the past, although never by an expert as this man obviously was. His hands rested possessively on her hips, holding her to him, the pressure of his mouth increasing now, becoming more demanding. And she wasn't able to meet that demand; her inexperience held her back.

Rick sensed her lack of response, raising his head to move savagely away from her. 'I told you I was insane,' he ground out. 'Now I've just proved it.'

She blinked hard to clear her head. 'How did you do that?' she asked huskily.

'Use your head, Robyn,' he snapped, running his hand through his already untidy hair. 'What I just did was totally out of character——'

'Kissing me?'

'Kissing the child you still are,' he corrected harshly. 'God, I have to get back to civilisation!'

She swallowed hard. 'But——'

'Would you leave?' He turned his back on her, his shoulders rigid.

'Rick——'

'*Now*, Robyn!'

'But your supper——' she said dazedly.

'I can see to that myself. Will you just go!' He raised his voice enough to make his point forcefully.

She went. What had *happened* in there? One minute they had been arguing as usual, the next Rick had been kissing her with a hunger that had made escape impossible. Not that she had really wanted to. That kiss had been devastating to her peace of mind, in fact she was still trembling from the contact of his hard body, his muscular thighs bruising against hers.

But he was hiding something, or from someone. Whichever it was he wasn't the ideal man to be attracted to. And she was attracted, had been since the moment she first saw him, blazing anger and all. The harshness, the bitterness, shielded the natural sensuality of his nature—that much had been obvious from the way he had kissed her just now. That he rarely gave in to that sensuality was also obvious.

She would be curious to know what work he had done before coming here, what sort of life he had led. Whatever it was it had been vastly different from the way he was living now.

'You're looking a little flushed, love,' her mother said worriedly when she arrived home a few minutes later.

Robyn blushed even more. 'It's just from the walk, Mum.'

Billy looked up from doing his homework on the dining-room table. 'Sure it isn't a case of loveitis?'

She frowned. 'A touch of——? No, it isn't!' she snapped angrily, blushing bright red after the intensity of the kiss Rick Howarth had just given her.

'I bet it is,' her brother taunted, sitting back in his

chair to eye her mockingly. 'What have you been doing over at Mr Howarth's place all this time?'

'Mind your own business!' Robyn said tautly.

Billy's interest quickened. 'Why are you so defensive if he didn't——'

'Shut up!' she ordered shrilly, still in a state of confusion, remembering firm lips on hers, the warmth of Rick Howarth's tongue as it ran tantalisingly over her sensitive lower lip. The memory of that was too private to share with anyone, especially her tormenting little brother.

'Robyn!' her mother reprimanded.

She bit her lip. 'I'm sorry, Mum. But he goaded me,' she glared at Billy.

'Boys will be boys,' her mother sighed.

And men would be men! And at the moment Rick Howarth was a man seriously in need of a woman. His impatience with her inexperience had been evidence enough that it wasn't really her he had been kissing, just a presentable female with a passable body. If he was married, as she suspected he was, then he would be used to—to a certain physical relationship, and that he was missing that relationship was obvious.

Billy grinned mischievously. 'I only wanted to know if you and Mr Howarth——'

'Billy!' his mother cut in. 'Take your books and do your homework upstairs.'

'Oh, but, Mum——'

'Go on,' she ordered. 'And you aren't going anywhere until it's finished.'

He collected up his books and moved to the door, poking his tongue out at Robyn as he moved out of sight of their mother. Robyn couldn't really blame him, though. Normally she could take any amount of his teasing without complaint, usually gave back as good as she got. But not tonight, and not about Rick Howarth, not when she was feeling so raw about him.

'Anything wrong?' her mother asked gently.

'Er—no. No, nothing is wrong,' she managed a casual shrug. 'I was a bit delayed getting back from Mr Howarth's because I—I offered to get him his supper. He's a bit helpless around a cooker.'

'So I noticed, by the food he ordered. Everything out of a tin or packet.' Her mother shook her head. 'It wouldn't do for your father.'

Robyn felt sure it didn't really 'do' for Rick either. There was an air about him, a feeling that he usually demanded and received perfection in everything. Oh, she wished she knew what the mystery was surrounding him!

They were particularly busy at the library the next day, this being the day for the local market, something guaranteed to bring more people into town, and consequently into the library. Robyn was on the check-out desk, stamping the books and taking in the cards, finding herself with a constant stream of people, so she was quite relieved when morning coffee-break came round, less pleased when she saw it was Selma and another girl in the staff-room.

'Did he come round last night?' Selma asked instantly.

Robyn wished, and not for the first time, that the other girl wouldn't take quite such an interest in her love-life. By all accounts Selma had enough trouble keeping up with her own stormy relationships, apparently having found herself yet another boy-friend. Besides, Robyn was conscious of Joan's interest in this conversation.

'No, he didn't,' she replied stiffly, pouring herself a cup of coffee.

Selma shrugged dismissively. 'Find yourself another one.'

She wished it were as simple as that. She just couldn't get Rick Howarth out of her mind. He said he had to get back to civilisation—did that mean he would be leaving today, have disappeared from Sanford as suddenly as he had appeared? She knew she didn't want him to do that, knew that for all her antagonism towards him she found him fascinating.

Things were still hectic after her break, and Mr Leaven took her off the front desk and put her on to tidying the non-fiction shelves. After Monday he seemed reluctant to allow her anywhere near the fiction section. He knew very well the medical section wouldn't interest her at all, especially when she dropped one of the huge volumes on her toe.

She swore loudly, receiving a reproving look from Mr Leaven as she picked up the book, muttering to herself as she replaced it on the top shelf.

'What did you say?' Selma stood behind her, eyeing her flushed face curiously.

'I said damn Oliver Pendleton. He wrote this book,' she explained. 'And I just crushed my toe with it.'

Selma tutted. 'Never mind that now. He's here,' she announced triumphantly.

Robyn frowned. 'Oliver Pendleton?' she asked in a puzzled voice.

'No, silly,' the other girl sighed her impatience. 'Your boy-friend, he's here.'

'Boy-friend?' She gulped. 'You mean——'

'Yes!' Selma pulled her along beside her. 'He just came to the enquiries desk,' she appeared not to notice Robyn's reluctance to follow her. 'As soon as he said his name I knew who he was.'

Yes, it really was him. Standing authoritatively by the main desk, an air of detachment about him, was Rick Howarth.

CHAPTER THREE

AFTER the way they had parted the evening before Robyn was unsure of Rick's reaction to seeing her again—after all, he had more or less thrown her out of his house. But she had a curious Selma looking on, obviously waiting for the big reunion.

'Well, go on!' Selma urged her forward.

There was nothing else for it, she would have to continue this charade—even though Rick wouldn't have the faintest idea what was going on and would probably expose her for the liar she was.

She swallowed hard and moved determinedly forward, seeing Rick's eyes narrow in recognition, his expression instantly one of wariness. 'Hello, darling,' she greeted huskily, colour flooding her cheeks at her use of the false endearment. 'If you've come to take me out to lunch you're a little early.' She looked at him appealingly, hoping he would understand her silent plea.

He hid his surprise very well, his gaze shifting momentarily to Selma as she stood several feet away from them, obviously listening avidly to their conversation, although trying to give the impression that she was interested solely in the row of books in front of her.

Rick's eyes flickered with something that looked like anger, and for a moment Robyn knew that he was going to denounce her as a liar. Then he smiled, a smile that didn't reach the hardness of his eyes, although that wasn't visible to anyone but her. 'I don't mind waiting,' he drawled deeply. 'After all, you're worth waiting for.' His eyes clearly mocked her now.

Her flush deepened, and she looked selfconsciously at

Selma. 'You can't wait for me here,' she told him abruptly. 'I—I'll meet you down at the café in the square in half an hour.' She held her breath as she waited for his reply.

'Okay,' he shrugged. 'Half an hour it is.' He nodded abruptly and was gone.

She began to breathe easily again. Rick had no reason to do so, and yet he had helped her out. But she doubted he would actually go to the café, he had only agreed to help her save face in front of Selma. She was very grateful to him, though, and would have to go round to his house tonight and thank him—and explain! Explaining her deceit wasn't going to be easy.

'He's *gorgeous*!' Selma said ecstatically, her eyes dreamy.

Rick had looked rather handsome today. He always did to her, but today his clothes, fitted brown trousers and shirt, a cream jerkin zipped partway up his chest, had been quite smart. His hair was still too long, of course, but didn't detract from his looks at all. Selma was right, he was gorgeous.

'I wish I could meet someone like him,' Selma added eagerly. 'Do you think he has a brother?'

'No. I—Well—He could have. I don't know,' Robyn finished lamely.

The other girls's eyes were wide. 'You don't?'

'No,' Robyn answered abruptly. 'We—we haven't really discussed his family.'

Selma grinned. 'I think I'd have better things to do when with a man like him too!'

Robyn blushed as the other girl's meaning became clear to her. 'Oh, I don't—We don't—I haven't known him very long,' she said awkwardly.

'With a man like that I shouldn't think you would need to.'

Her gaze sharpened. She didn't like the way Selma

kept referring to Rick. 'A man like that?' she queried
tautly.

Selma smiled. 'Well, he isn't likely to want to just sit
and hold your hand, now is he?'

No, he wasn't, she had known that from the hard
demand of his kiss. There could be no gentle prolonged
wooing with this man, he was far too experienced to
accept such an insipid relationship.

Robyn turned to leave; she still had the Art section to
tidy. 'I have to get back to work,' she said stiffly. 'And I
think you'd better do the same,' she added with a warning look in Mr Leaven's direction.

Selma grimaced. 'I don't think he was ever young,'
she muttered, but went back to work anyway.

Only half Robyn's mind was on what she was doing
now, her thoughts all of Rick. What had he been doing
here? The obvious answer was that he had come to take
out a book!—but he hadn't left with one. But he hadn't
come to see her either, because although the emotion
had been quickly masked he had been surprised to see
her here. She would ask him tonight, fully intending to
go to Orchard House and thank him for his help.

When the time came for her to go to lunch she knew
she would have to go out or arouse Selma's suspicions,
although it was her usual practice to have a read in the
staff-room.

Curiosity took her round to the coffee shop in the
square, hating the rush and bustle of the people as they
pushed roughly past her on their way to the market. As
she had known, Rick wasn't outside the café, and although she had been expecting it she still felt a sense of
disappointment.

'Let's get out of here,' he suddenly muttered beside
her, scowling at the crowds of people.

Robyn blinked up at him, her eyes as huge as pansies.
'Rick . . .' she said stupidly.

His mouth twisted. 'Your powers of deduction are amazing,' he scorned. 'You told me to be here and here I am.'

'But I—I didn't mean it,' she said haltingly.

'I know that, *darling*,' he mocked. 'And when we get away from here you can explain exactly what you did mean. If your youthful body is wondering when it's next going to be fed,' he taunted, 'I have your lunch right here.' He held up two paper bags and two cans of Coke. 'Ham salad rolls and fresh cream cakes.'

'Chocolate éclair?' she asked hopefully, not wanting to appear too eager to fall in with this unexpected bonus of his company during the day.

His harsh features relaxed into a smile. 'I must be psychic.' He took her elbow, leading her away from the market and into a back street where he had parked the Jaguar.

She settled comfortably into the luxury of her leather seat, feeling rather like a cat who had been given a saucer of cream. The delivery van and car her father could run to were nowhere near the class of this car; its interior was even more impressive than its exterior.

'There's a park not far from here,' she told Rick as he climbed in beside her.

'The food is for eating, not feeding to the ducks.' He drove smoothly and without effort, as much in control of this powerful vehicle as he appeared to be of everything else.

Robyn felt good just to be sitting next to him, shooting him shy glances from beneath lowered lashes. There was an air of distinction about him even in the casual clothes he always wore, a stamp of authority, an aura of power and the knowledge of knowing what to do with that power.

'I'm only on a light diet,' he drawled suddenly. 'I don't intend eating you.' He gave her a mocking glance. 'So you can stop looking at me so apprehensively.'

'I wasn't——'

'Oh yes, you were,' Rick insisted grimly. 'And maybe I've given you reason to feel that way. Last night——'

'I'd rather not talk about it,' she told him stiffly; the way he had rejected her was still painful to think about.

His hand moved to rest momentarily on her knee, burning her skin through the thin material of her skirt. 'We have to talk about it.' His hand returned to the steering-wheel.

'Why do we?' Robyn sighed. 'Nothing happened.'

'I *kissed* you!'

'So?' She looked at him challengingly. 'I've been kissed before.'

'Have you?' he taunted.

'Yes!' Her eyes flashed. 'I may not be as experienced as you——'

His harsh laugh cut her off. 'No, you aren't,' he scorned.

'It's nothing to boast about,' she snapped indignantly.

Rick drew the car to a halt in the car space near the park, turning in his seat to look at her. 'I'm not boasting, Robyn, merely being practical.'

'Practical!' she repeated disgustedly.

'Yes, practical.' He wrenched her chin round, forcing her to look at him. 'What do you want with an old man like me?' he rasped.

'Old——!' Her mouth twitched with humour, and she finally burst out laughing. 'Now you're being ridiculous,' she chuckled.

Rick gave a rueful smile. 'Maybe I am. But the first dirty-old-man look I get and I'm bringing you straight back to the car.'

She was just relieved to be spending this time with

him, her hand in his as they walked through the park to the pond.

'What were you doing at the library this morning?' she asked interestedly.

'Looking for a book.' He shrugged. 'They didn't have it.' He gave her a reproving look as she fed half her roll to the waiting ducks.

'I'll eat all my cake,' she promised.

'Here you are, then,' and he handed her one of the two fresh cream doughnuts.

She frowned her disappointment. 'You said it was a chocolate éclair,' she pouted.

Rick grinned. 'No, I didn't, I just said I was psychic.'

'You cheated!'

He quirked one eyebrow. 'So?'

'So—nothing,' she smiled at him, obediently eating the cake. 'I like doughnuts too.'

'I thought you might,' he said dryly, flicking cream off the end of her nose.

Robyn blushed as an elderly couple walked by, their expressions ones of smiling indulgence.

'They probably think I'm your father,' Rick muttered.

She looked at him challengingly. 'Then prove that you aren't.'

'Prove——?' He frowned, eyeing her suspiciously. 'Are you asking me to kiss you?'

'Yes,' she answered calmly, surprised at her own audacity.

'You cheeky little devil!'

'Well?'

'Okay,' he shrugged. 'Whatever you want.'

This time she was prepared for his lips on hers, and opened her mouth to accept his full passion, her arms up about his neck, her hands in the dark thickness of his hair. He was gentler with her today, although no less demanding, his arms like steel bands as he strained her closer to him.

He moved back, his eyes a warm caressing grey. 'Was that satisfactory, madam?' he taunted mockingly.

She was shaken by that kiss, physically moved, but she knew Rick was striving for lightness, so her mood matched his own. 'It could have been better,' she told him casually.

'Not in a public park, surely?' he drawled.

She pretended to give it some thought, although her lips still tingled from their contact with his. 'Possibly not,' she agreed.

Rick stood up, pulling her to her feet too, and moved to the litter-bin to dispose of the debris from their meal. 'Definitely not,' he turned to say firmly. 'And don't ask again, young lady, I find it difficult to say no to you.'

She gave him an innocent look. 'I was only trying to show that elderly couple that you aren't my father, uncle, or older brother.'

'I think you more than did that.' He scowled. 'You have yet to tell me what that charade at the library was all about,' he reminded her darkly.

'Ah,' she blushed guiltily, biting her lip. 'Do we have to talk about that?'

'I think so,' Rick insisted firmly. 'After all, that is the reason I'm here.'

'The only reason?'

'Well, I doubt you would have invited me out to lunch otherwise,' he said dryly. 'So tell me.'

She began reluctantly, finishing in a rush as she saw his face darken ominously. It wasn't something that put her in a very good light, and she knew he had a right to be angry with her.

'Why me?' he demanded harshly.

Robyn bit her lip. 'I didn't know anyone else.'

He frowned. 'In other words I was convenient.

Someone who actually did exist if your friend Selma bothered to make enquiries, someone new to the area and so unlikely to be questioned myself about dating you.'

'Yes,' she admitted miserably.

His eyes were narrowed. 'Why?'

She frowned her puzzlement. 'I just told you——'

'Not that,' Rick dismissed impatiently. 'Why don't you have a boy-friend?'

She shrugged. 'I just don't.'

'Have you ever?'

'Of course I—No,' she corrected softly. 'Not really.'

'Why not?'

She flushed her resentment. 'I just haven't! It isn't a crime, is it?' she flashed angrily.

'That depends.' He pursed his mouth thoughtfully.

'Depends?' she echoed sharply.

'On the reason for it.' His gaze ran slowly over her youthful curves. 'Are you frightened of a man's possession?'

Her eyes widened at the intimacy of such a question. Admittedly she had become closer to Rick during the last hour, was starting to like him more than could be good for her, but she would never have dreamt of asking him such a personal question. Not that it would ever be necessary—this man feared nothing, certainly not physical relationships.

'Are you?' he repeated coldly.

That was it, the question was asked coldly, clinically, as if it interested him in an impersonal way. 'No!' Robyn snapped. 'If you must know, sex bores me.' She looked at him challengingly.

'Really?' he asked dryly. 'And how do you know that when you've never tried it?'

'I didn't say that!' She turned on her heel and began walking back to the car.

Her disappointment was acute when Rick made no

effort to catch up with her, but followed at a more leisurely pace, arriving at the car several minutes after her,
still in no hurry as he unlocked the car doors.

'I have to get back to work,' she told him waspishly.

'You still have ten minutes,' he informed her calmly.
'Plenty of time to get you back.'

She kept shooting him resentful glances as the Jaguar
ate up the distance back to the library. Why didn't he
say something, question her about that last comment
she had made before walking off? Probably because it
didn't really interest him. Oh dear, she had bored him
now! Why couldn't she learn to keep her mouth shut?

'One good turn deserves another,' he said suddenly.
'How about cooking my dinner this evening?' He
quirked one eyebrow enquiringly.

She was so relieved that he wanted to see her again
that refusing didn't even enter her head. She had been
feeling miserable and now she felt elated. 'I'd love to,'
she agreed shakily, wishing she didn't sound quite so
eager but unable to stop herself. 'Although I—I can't
actually cook,' she revealed reluctantly.

Humour lightened his harsh features. 'You mean your
mother hasn't passed on any of her talent?'

'None at all, I'm afraid,' she told him with a grimace.

'Then we'll pick up some Chinese from the takeaway
in Ampthull. Do you like Chinese?'

She would like raw whalemeat if it meant she could be
with him! 'I love it!' Although that was a slight exaggera-
tion she had enjoyed it on the one occasion she had tried
sweet and sour chicken from this same restaurant.

Rick nodded. 'Shall I call for you or will you walk
down?'

'I'll walk down,' she told him hastily. On the few oc-
casions when a boy had called for her at her home her
father had asked him such personal questions that she
wasn't surprised when she was brought home as early as

possible and no mention of a further date was forth-
coming. Goodness, they had only wanted to take her
out for a drink or to the cinema, they weren't there to
ask for her hand in marriage!

Rick got out of the car to come round and open her
door for her, bending down to kiss her lightly on the
lips. 'Just in case your friend happened to be watching,'
he drawled as she blushed fiery red.

She looked down at her feet, cursing her gaucheness
when she was with this worldly man. 'I'll see you about
seven, then,' she said huskily.

'Seven it is,' he agreed abruptly, making no further
attempt to touch her but getting into his car and driving
off.

Robyn stood on the pavement for several moments
after he had driven off. Somehow she had become deeply
attracted to Rick Howarth, she who had never been
particularly interested in any particular boy before. *Boy!*
Rick was far from that, his confidence with women was
as obvious as his dark good looks.

'Hey, Robyn,' Selma hissed in her ear. 'It's time to
get back to work.'

Robyn blushed as she realised how stupid she must
look just standing here gazing into space, the Jaguar
long since having disappeared. 'I was deep in thought,'
she said awkwardly, walking beside the other girl as they
entered the library.

Selma giggled. 'I could see that. Dazed would be a
more apt description. I wish I'd met him first,' she added
wistfully.

Perhaps Rick would too if he knew that Selma would
have absolutely no qualms about entering into the intimate relationship he obviously craved. Besides, Selma
was four years older than she was, and wouldn't be
considered the child he still thought her.

'Well, you didn't,' she snapped resentfully. 'And Rick

happens to be *my* boy-friend.' She was deeply ashamed
of her behaviour as soon as the words had left her lips.
'I'm sorry, Selma,' she was instantly contrite. 'I didn't
mean to be rude.'

The other girl grinned goodnaturedly. 'That's okay. I
wouldn't welcome your interest either if he was mine.'

'All the same——'

'Miss Castle,' a familiar authoritative voice interrupted them, 'I wonder if I might have a word with you?'

Although uttered in the form of a request Mr
Leaven's words were an order nonetheless, and both
girls knew that. Selma hurried off, obviously feeling
relieved to escape whatever reprimand was coming now.

'Miss Castle,' Mr Leaven repeated in an icy voice, 'it
has never been my practice to encourage—friends of the
staff to call for them here. And I certainly do not con-
done that—display of affection that took place right
outside the library doors.'

Deep colour flooded her cheeks. 'I——'

'There can be no excuse for such a display in public,'
he rapped out. 'See that it doesn't happen again.'

'I told you, he's never been young,' Selma remarked
later when told of the incident.

Robyn was aware of Mr Leaven's disapproval all day,
and was glad to get home that evening, although she
felt very young and uncomfortable as she explained to
her parents that she was having dinner with Rick.

Her mother frowned. 'You're seeing rather a lot of
him, dear.'

She flushed. 'Don't you like him?'

'It isn't that——'

'What your mother is trying to say,' her father interrupted, 'is that we find your transformation from
tomboy to girlish infatuation for an older man rather
too sudden for comfort.'

'Peter!'

He flushed angrily. 'Well, I don't like the man——'

'You don't know him, Peter. He's always seemed very nice when he's been in the shop.'

'Well, of course he has,' her husband dismissed. 'They all do. But you can hardly get to know someone across a shop counter. I don't think you should see him so much, Robyn.'

She blushed. 'This will only be the third time.'

'In as many days,' her father scowled. 'The next thing I know you'll be coming to me telling me you're in trouble.'

'Peter!'

'Daddy . . .!'

'All right, all right, I admit I may be going a bit far,' he said uncomfortably. 'But what do we know of the man? He turned up here three weeks ago to rent Orchard House, and——'

'Rent it?' Robyn asked sharply. 'He's only renting it?'

Her father nodded. 'So Mrs Reed told me, and she should know—she knows everything. Besides, he has all his mail sent here, says Orchard House is only a temporary address. You didn't know that either, did you?'

'No . . .'

'You know nothing about the man at all!'

Her head went high, her expression rebellious. 'I know that I like him. And it isn't girlish infatuation I feel for him, it isn't anything—yet. But it could be—if well-meaning people like you would mind their own business!' She turned and ran out of the house, brushing past Billy as he arrived home after his football practice.

'Hey, watch where you're going!' he complained as she knocked his holdall out of his hand.

'I'm sorry,' she choked, bending down to pick up the bag, tears glistening on her cheeks as she raised her head.

Billy frowned. 'Hey, you're crying!'

'No, I'm not.' She brushed the tears away with the back of her hand. 'I'll see you later.' She gave him a tremulous smile before hurriedly leaving the house.

Her father had never spoken that way to her before. And all because she wanted to see Rick!

She didn't even wait for Rick to answer the door once she arrived at Orchard House, bursting into the kitchen to find it empty. She could hear the sound of pounding typewriter keys, and remembering the one she had seen in Rick's bedroom she ran up the stairs.

'Rick! Rick?' she called before throwing open the bedroom door and going inside. 'Oh, Rick!' she cried before launching herself into his arms as he stood up.

'What's the matter?' he demanded roughly, his arms tightening about her.

'Nothing now,' she sobbed. 'Just hold me!' She buried herself against his chest, finding his shirt partly unbuttoned, her cheek against his hair-roughened skin.

He took a firm hold of her arms, holding her away from him. 'You have to tell me what's wrong if you want me to help you,' he told her gruffly.

'I don't want help, I want—I want you to kiss me, Rick.' She looked up at him with huge pleading blue eyes, her vulnerable mouth parted invitingly, her hands clinging to the broad width of his shoulders.

He frowned darkly. 'I have no intention of doing anything until I know what the hell is going on.'

She sniffed inelegantly. 'First Mr Leaven, my boss, told me not to meet you at the library, then my father— my father—He said—He implied——'

'What?' Rick rasped, his fingers biting painfully into her upper arms. 'What did he say, Robyn?'

There were two bright spots of colour in her cheeks. 'Terrible things,' she shuddered.

Rick shook her, his mouth set impatiently. 'Tell me!'

'He said—he said——' she hiccuped back the tears.

'He wasn't very nice about you, and he—he implied that you and I—that in a couple of months——'

'That I could get you pregnant?' he finished incredulously, the tension leaving him and humour starting to take over. 'Is that what he said?' Rick sounded really amused now.

'Yes, he did!' She was indignant at his reaction to something that had upset her very deeply. 'And I didn't find it in the least funny.'

'Perhaps it wouldn't be,' he released her, 'if it were even a possibility,' he finished insultingly.

Robyn stiffened. 'Meaning it isn't?'

'Not in the least,' he dismissed calmly. 'I have no intention of going to bed with you.'

'It may not be intended,' she flashed.

His mouth quirked with humour. 'Meaning I may become so overwhelmed with desire for you that I won't be able to stop myself?'

'You could be!' she snapped.

Rick shook his head. 'Never. I learnt how to control those sort of urges years ago. That sort of immaturity belongs to boys and besotted idiots—of which I am neither.'

Robyn went very white. 'You make it all sound so—so cold.'

'It is.'

'You mean you just—decide when you want to make love and—and do it? There's no clamouring of the senses, no—no——'

'Sudden urge to possess one particular woman?' he finished dryly. 'Not in my case, no. Oh, I enjoy sex as much as the next man, more than some, probably, but it doesn't rule my life as it does some men's, doesn't control me.'

Robyn bit her lip. 'You make it sound—not very nice.' She pulled a face.

'Coming from someone who this afternoon told me she found sex boring I find your criticism a little surprising,' he said mockingly. 'Besides, I've always found the sexual act very enjoyable, I just don't let it rule me, I rule *it*.'

'You've never been in love, have you?'

His mouth twisted. 'Meaning you have.'

'No,' she shook her head, 'I haven't. You just don't sound as if you've ever loved.'

'Well, I have!' he rasped. 'Now let's get out of my bedroom. It's hardly the place to be having this sort of conversation.'

'It seems ideal to me.'

'Well, it isn't,' he scowled. 'I may just decide to prove to you that you can enjoy sex without loving someone.'

Robyn blushed. 'You—you were typing when I came in,' she changed the subject. 'Is that your work?'

His mouth set in a thin angry line. 'Who says I work?'

'Well, you must do something!'

'At the moment I'm mainly trying to cope with the hysterics and inquisitiveness of a rather nosey young girl. Now let's go downstairs,' and he pushed her out of the room, following close behind her.

'I was only——'

'You were asking a lot of questions that I have no intention of supplying answers to,' he told her coldly. 'And just for the record, your father was right to be concerned about you, you're too damned trusting with a man you've only known a few days. You were alone with me in my bedroom just now, and your words and actions could have been taken for ones of invitation——'

'They weren't meant to be!' she cut in indignantly, knowing that she wasn't telling the whole truth. She had thrown herself at this man, shamelessly, and he had rejected her.

'Maybe not,' Rick shrugged. 'Even so, you had little protection up there with me. You're lucky my tastes don't run to bright-eyed teenagers.'

'Aren't I?' she said sarcastically, feeling as if she could have hit him in that moment. 'And you're just lucky my taste isn't for cold-blooded, ageing Romeos,' she added insultingly, still smarting from his rejection.

His mouth tightened, but he didn't cut into her verbally as she had expected him to. 'Make your mind up,' he drawled. 'I can either be cold-blooded or a Romeo, never both.'

'*You* are.'

He ruffled her hair, throwing her blonde hair into disorder. 'Calm down, little girl,' he taunted. 'All this emotion in one evening will tire you out.'

'Stop talking to me as if I were a child!'

'Then stop acting like one!'

She looked at the tight line of his well-shaped mouth, realising he was coming to the end of his patience with her. He would throw her out again if she weren't careful. 'I'm hungry,' she muttered in a sulky voice.

Rick grinned. 'Then we'll go out and get the food. And don't take what your father said so much to heart. Better a warning before than after.'

'But you said——'

He sighed. 'I meant with any man, not with me.'

'You're insulting!' she gasped.

'Sensible, Robyn,' he corrected, opening the back door for her to exit. 'Come on, I'm hungry too.'

'Why are you bothering with me?' she asked moodily as they drove to Ampthull.

He gave her a sideways glance. 'In what way?'

She flushed her irritation. 'In any way. If you don't want to—to——'

'Sleep with you,' he finished dryly. 'You can't even say it, let alone do it,' he derided. 'And I don't want to sleep with you.'

'Then what do you want?'

'Company.'

Her eyes widened. 'Company?'

He shrugged. 'I've been alone a lot the last few months. Meeting you, talking to you, has made me realise that like most human beings I crave company now and again. Besides, you were the one who instigated our first meeting today.'

'I didn't expect you to turn up!'

'Sorry!' His mouth twisted. 'You should have made that clear to me and then we could have forgotten the whole thing.'

She was behaving childishly, she knew that, and it would serve her right if he stopped the car and made her get out without giving her any dinner. 'I'm sorry,' she muttered awkwardly. 'I'm behaving badly.'

'You are. But maybe you can be excused that after the battering you must have taken from your father this evening. I'll see if I can find the time to go into the shop tomorrow and reassure him that I don't have evil designs on his daughter's body.'

'Meaning that you think of me as a daughter yourself,' she flashed.

Rick's mouth tightened. 'You know damn well I don't. I could easily lose myself in you, enjoy you, but it wouldn't get us anywhere. I'd like you as a friend, Robyn, a *young* friend.'

And she didn't want him as a friend at all. He was attractive, dangerously so, very exciting to be with, and certainly not the sort of material friends were made of.

'It's that or nothing,' he put in harshly at her continued silence.

'Maybe I would prefer nothing.'

'That's your prerogative,' he told her stiffly. 'For God's sake stop cheapening yourself!' he added tautly.

'I wasn't——'

'Yes, you were, damn you! What's the matter, aren't there enough young men in the area? Do you have to throw yourself at a complete stranger to get the attention you crave?'

'I didn't,' she said defensively.

'I don't know what else you would call it,' Rick dismissed disgustedly.

'If that's the opinion you have of me then you might as well drop me off now,' she choked.

'I just might do that!' he threatened grimly.

'Well, go on, then!' she ordered shrilly.

'Robyn——'

'Go on!' she interrupted his patiently reasoning voice, feeling very raw at the moment; today had been a day of reprimands and rejection. 'You're right, after all, why should I bother with someone like you when there are plenty of *boys* I could be going out with?'

Rick's face darkened angrily. 'You're one of the most unreasonable females——'

'And you're the rudest man I've ever met!' she glared at him.

'Robyn——' again he tried to reason with her.

'Will you stop this car and let me out!' Two bright spots of angry colour brightened her cheeks.

'I'll stop the car!' It ground to a halt and Rick turned savagely in his seat. 'You're the most exasperating girl——!' He pulled her roughly towards him, grinding his mouth down on hers, forcing her lips apart in a kiss that was purely motivated by anger.

Even so Robyn responded—until his fierceness began to frighten her, the singleminded purpose behind the kiss

making her pull away from him to stare up at him with
wide apprehensive eyes.

His expression was grim, his jaw rigid; a pulse beat
angrily in his throat, his grey eyes were steely. 'Was that
what you wanted?' he bit out contemptuously. 'Because
if it is there's plenty more where that came from!'

'No!' Robyn's face was stricken as she hastily pushed
open the car door. 'I'm sorry I ever came near you.' She
scrambled inelegantly out on to the side of the road.

'So am I,' he snapped, putting the car into gear and
accelerating away from her with a screech of the car
tyres.

She made her way miserably back home, aware of the
fact that she had made a fool out of herself. Rick
Howarth saw her only as a child to be amusing, someone
to brighten up a dull evening for him. The fact that she
was attracted to him meant nothing to him, and why
should it? Even the few kisses he had given her had
shown her she was out of his league. He would have a
beautiful woman somewhere in his life, possibly even
the wife she had first suspected him of having, and a
naïve impressionable girl of eighteen was hardly likely
to be of any interest to him.

He had wanted her as a friend, and a friend was one
thing she could never be to him, too aware of his sensuality to ever settle for complacency, too attracted to
him to settle for mere companionship.

Not that she was even being offered that now! Rick
had rejected all of her feeble attempts to show him how
attractive she found him, and she wouldn't make a fool
of herself like that again.

Her mother was in the lounge when she got home,
and she looked up anxiously as Robyn entered the room.
'All right, love?' she queried gently.

'Yes, thanks, Mum.' She choked back the tears.

'About what your dad said earlier——'

'It's all right,' she dismissed. 'It isn't important.' And strangely enough it wasn't any more. Her father had merely been acting protectively, she understood that now.

'Of course it is,' her mother insisted. 'Your dad is so upset. He didn't mean it quite the way it sounded. It's just that he can see the pitfalls you perhaps can't see yourself.'

Robyn gave a brittle fixed smile. 'Well, he needn't worry any more. I'm not going to see Mr Howarth again.'

Her mother looked concerned. 'It isn't because of anything your father said, is it?'

'No,' she shook her head firmly, 'nothing Dad said.' But plenty Rick himself had said!

CHAPTER FOUR

SHE saw the light blue Jaguar several times during the next few weeks, but fortunately Rick never seemed to see her. Unless that was intentional! Maybe he was deliberately avoiding her.

Well, his luck held out for three weeks, and then quite by chance he came into the shop one Thursday morning as Robyn was helping out during her day off from the library. He looked taken aback at first, although the emotion was quickly masked.

'Good morning, Mr Howarth,' she greeted stiffly. 'Can I get you anything?'

'My mail,' he replied tersely, looking as gaunt and unkempt as he had the first time she had seen him.

She looked under the counter for the single thick envelope her father had kept for him, wondering if Rick could possibly be feeding himself. He hadn't bought any groceries lately, that she knew from her mother, which had prompted her mother to send Billy over with a couple of stews and casseroles. The plates had always come back clean and empty, and yet Rick didn't look as if he were really eating them.

Robyn at once cursed herself for her concern. What Rick Howarth did, in any shape or form, was none of her business—he had made that patently obvious.

She held out the envelope, watching as he ripped it open to take out several smaller envelopes. He flicked through the contents, his expression darkening as he reached a delicate blue envelope, its perfume discernible even across the width of the counter.

'Damn!' Robyn heard him mutter under his breath.

'What's the matter?' she taunted. 'Has she caught up with you?'

His eyes were glacial as he looked up at her. 'She?' he echoed in a chilling voice.

'Your wife,' Robyn guessed daringly.

'I have no wife!' he rasped.

'Girl-friend, then,' she shrugged as if it didn't really interest her who the writer of that perfumed letter was, or what she meant in his life. But she did care! Even after several weeks of not seeing him his attraction was as strong for her, the fluttering in her stomach, the nervous pulse-rate. Not that he was troubled by any of these symptoms; he was still glaring at the blue envelope in his hand.

He looked up, his mouth twisting. 'I don't have one of those either.' He stowed the letters away in the back pocket of the tight denims he wore. 'Robyn——'

'Excuse me, Mr Howarth,' she interrupted briskly. 'I have to serve Miss Stevens.' She had noticed the other woman in the shop even if he hadn't.

'That's all right, dear,' the gentle-voiced spinster turned to say. 'I'm just debating which shampoo to buy.'

Robyn came out from behind the counter. 'Perhaps I can help you choose.' Although no shampoo they stocked could help this elderly lady's loss of hair.

'But Mr Howarth——'

'Has finished,' Robyn said firmly. She picked up a bottle of the shampoo she always used herself. 'Why don't you try this one?' She pointedly ignored Rick as he still stood to one side glowering at her.

He didn't move for several more minutes, then with an angry sigh he turned on his heel and slammed out of the shop. Robyn instantly relaxed, concentrating all her attention on Miss Stevens's short shopping list, her main item being the tins of food for her two cats.

'I hope I didn't push in front of Mr Howarth,' Miss Stevens worried as she paid for her shopping.

'Not at all,' Robyn assured her tightly as she handed over her shopping. 'He merely called in for his mail, and he already had that.'

'Oh, I see.' The middle-aged woman eyed her enquiringly. 'Only I thought he was a friend of yours.'

Robyn gave her a startled look. 'Not particularly,' she evaded, returning her attention back to the tins she had been stacking on the shelves when Rick came in.

'Mrs Reed said that you and Mr Howarth were— well, that you visited him at his home.'

She flushed, having forgotten that Sarah Reed, the village gossip, lived next door to Miss Stevens. What Mrs Reed didn't know usually wasn't worth knowing, and she enjoyed nothing more than relaying the latest bit of gossip to anyone who would listen. Although Robyn was surprised Miss Stevens had been a recipient to this tittle tattle.

'Not that I take a lot of notice of what Sarah Reed has to say,' Miss Stevens instantly confirmed her thoughts. 'She always did talk a lot of nonsense, even at school. No, it was just that I happened to see you leaving Mr Howarth's house one evening a few weeks ago.'

'I went for my mother,' Robyn said abruptly. 'She doesn't think he feeds himself.'

'Neither do I. And he's such a handsome man. He looks as if he should have a wife.'

'Perhaps he has,' Robyn agreed noncommitally, knowing she had been relieved beyond words when Rick had denied having a wife. He had made his lack of interest in her patently clear, and yet to know he was married would put him completely out of her reach, and she wouldn't like that. It was silly to still be attracted to him, and yet she couldn't help herself. Maybe it was the memory of the potency of his kiss, whatever the reason her heart skipped a beat every time she saw him.

Miss Stevens left without pressing her any further, anxious to get back to her cats, two self-satisfied creatures who ruled the Stevens household with a twitch of their whiskers.

'Will you take Mr Howarth's supper over this evening?' Robyn's mother asked her later. 'Only Billy said he would be late back from school tonight.'

Her brother had been taking meals over to Rick Howarth for the past few weeks, her mother seeming to understand her own reluctance to go over there. 'I don't want to go,' Robyn told her bluntly, tidying away their own washed dishes.

'Now look, love——'

'I can't, Mum,' she said pleadingly. 'I thought you understood that after what happened——'

'I don't know what happened,' her mother prompted gently.

Robyn looked away, hot colour flooding her cheeks. 'Not a lot, really. I just—I can't face him again. I—I made rather a fool of myself over him. I think I embarrassed him.' She didn't think it, she *knew* it! She wasn't used to hiding her feelings, didn't go in for those sort of sophisticated games, and it hadn't occurred to her to act any differently with Rick. Her parents had always brought her up to do and say the honest thing, and showing Rick she liked him had been the honest thing— it had also been her downfall. Well, she wasn't going to fall into that trap again; if cool disinterest was what Rick wanted then that was what he was going to get in future, if there was any future for them.

'As bad as that?' her mother said softly at the distress on Robyn's face.

'Worse!' she grimaced. 'I just can't go, Mum.'

'Okay, love, I'll pop in on my way to Mrs Blewett's. She's got some material and a pattern to make a dress for her young granddaughter, and I said I'd go round tonight and collect them.'

Her mother often helped the elderly lady out in this way; Mrs Blewett's eyesight not as good as it had been. Besides, it gave them both a chance to have a chat.

It wasn't all that late when her mother returned, the dress pattern and pretty flowered material in her hand.

'Have a nice time?' Robyn asked guardedly.

Her mother sat down, putting her feet up on the stool with a sigh. 'It's such a shame to see what old age does to people. I remember Mrs Blewett being a sprightly thing when we first moved into the village. She certainly can't be called sprightly now, it takes her all of her time to get out of her chair.

Robyn's question hadn't really been directed at Mrs Blewett, much as she liked the old lady, but she couldn't ask outright about Rick, not without revealing how interested in him she was.

'Mr Howarth doesn't look at all well to me,' her mother frowned her concern.

Robyn's brow creased, recalling how white and drawn Rick had looked this morning. 'He doesn't?'

Her mother shook her head. 'But then that's to be expected. Orchard House isn't exactly the ideal place to be living. It must be damp, for one thing. And I don't suppose Mr Howarth has any heating there.'

'He has a fire in his bedroom,' Robyn told her absently.

'Does he, dear?' Her mother raised one eyebrow questioningly.

Colour flooded her cheeks as she shrugged. 'It was the only room with any furniture,' she explained lamely. 'I just happened to notice it.'

'Of course,' her mother accepted smoothly, although

Robyn could see she was still worried.

'That's the truth, Mum,' she insisted.

'I'm sure it is, dear. He asked after you,' her mother added softly.

'He did?' She couldn't even begin to hide her eager pleasure.

'Mm. He seemed concerned that you hadn't been back to visit him. He mentioned that you'd had an argument.'

Robyn bit her lip. 'Did he say what about?'

Her mother shook her head. 'Just that it was something petty.'

Petty! Oh, if only it had been! But perhaps to Rick it had been. His words to her mother seemed to imply that the incident had been forgotten by him. Had her rudeness this morning also been forgotten?

'He would like you to go round tomorrow if you have time,' her mother told her casually.

This did seem to indicate that Rick was willing to overlook her behaviour this morning too. 'I—er—I suppose I could go round in the evening.' She made her words as casual as she could in her excitement.

Her mother nodded. 'I think Mr Howarth might like that.'

'Really?'

'Really,' her mother nodded. 'He seems very lonely, Robyn.'

Just her luck that the back tyre on her bicycle burst on the ride home the next evening. One minute she had been pedalling happily along the road, eager to get home, eat her dinner and get over to Rick's, the next minute there was a thumping noise as her back tyre flattened to the rim, and the whole thing wobbled precariously.

'Damn!' she muttered as she climbed off to look helplessly down at the flat tyre.

She had only gone as far as the outskirts of Ampthull, which meant she still had almost three miles to go. She would never get to Rick's tonight now. It had been her late night at the library, and was past eight now. By the time she had walked home it would be after nine, much too late to go over to Rick's then.

'Damn, damn, damn!' she muttered again, beginning the long weary walk home.

Only a few cars passed her on the long country road, and none of them were familiar. She was very late, and surprised that her father hadn't come out looking for her. Her father had always worried about her if she wasn't home on time. She remembered one embarrassing occasion when she and another girl had met two boys in town and agreed to go for a coffee with them, her father had suddenly appeared in the café, his concern rapidly giving way to anger.

But even he didn't appear tonight, and as she had predicted, it was after nine when she reached home. Her mother was surprised to see her flushed and harassed face. Robyn mumbled an explanation, having no appetite for the dinner her mother put down on the table for her.

Her mother frowned. 'I never thought—I just thought you'd gone straight to Mr Howarth's from work.'

'I wouldn't do that,' she gasped.

'Not normally, no, but I thought . . . Never mind,' she smiled brightly. 'You're back now.'

'But it's too late,' Robyn said sulkily.

'To visit Mr Howarth? Yes, I suppose it is. But you can always go and see him tomorrow.'

She didn't want to see him tomorrow, she wanted to see him today. But she couldn't, and it was all the stupid bicycle's fault, the bicycle that had been the reason they had first met, and was now the reason they couldn't. 'I think the tyre from your bike must have perished,' she told her mother.

'Probably,' she nodded. 'It was quite old. Eat your dinner, Robyn.'

She ate with great reluctance, mainly to please her mother, certainly not because of any real desire for the food.

'Your father has gone to the school to watch Billy play football,' her mother explained his absence. 'So he wouldn't have been here to come and collect you even if we had realised there was something wrong.'

Robyn pushed away her half-eaten meal with an apologetic smile. 'I suppose I can always go over to Orchard House tomorrow evening.' Although that seemed a very long time away.

'I'm sure Mr Howarth will understand, although I did mention to him earlier that you might find the time to go over for a few minutes——'

'Oh, Mum!' she giggled. 'You didn't say that, did you?'

'Exactly that.'

'Oh, Mum!' There was a certain amount of dismay in her voice now.

Her mother smiled. 'Never be too eager, Robyn, especially with a man like that. He won't appreciate it, believe me.'

'Is that how you got Dad, by playing hard to get?'

Her mother looked coy. 'Sometimes you have to be devious.'

Robyn felt happier after that, enjoying a generous portion of the trifle her mother had made for dessert. Her mother had just endorsed her idea of playing it cool where Rick was concerned, and maybe tomorrow wouldn't be so long coming after all.

It just wasn't her week! She missed the bus by seconds the next morning; for once it had arrived early, and it was half an hour later before her father could be spared from the shop to take her into Ampthull. She telephoned

Mr Leaven and told him of her expected lateness, receiving a cool reception from him. Not that she could blame him; her work, when she did arrive on time, hadn't really been up to standard the last few weeks. She had been constantly brooding about Rick, longing to go and see him but expecting only contempt from him if she did.

She was almost an hour late getting to the library, and Mr Leaven's disapproving frown wasn't exactly undeserved. If she had been at the bus stop at the right time, instead of expecting the bus to be the five or ten minutes late it usually was, then she wouldn't have missed it.

'You'll have to stay on tonight and make up for this lateness,' Mr Leaven warned her.

Staying on would mean she would miss the only bus home, and as tonight was the late night opening for the shop her father wouldn't be able to call for her. That meant another three-mile walk. And another late night home. It was the latter she hated; it seemed everything was against her going to see Rick!

Just her luck that it should start to rain when she got halfway to Sanford. Probably her father would come out for her now, and perhaps he would have mended her bicycle for tomorrow. Thank goodness the day after that was Sunday. She was going to need that day off to get over this week.

She was absolutely drenched before she got much farther, and she promised herself that she would accept the next lift offered to her, having turned down two offers already, the memory of her mother's dark warnings about accepting lifts from strangers still with her from a child.

But she was sure when her mother had given the warning that she hadn't taken into account the fact that she was likely to catch pneumonia if she didn't take the next lift that came her way.

The arc of the approaching headlights picked out the light raincoat she wore, and the car swished to a halt several yards behind her. Even in this dull light of the heavy rain it was possible to pick out the light blue Jaguar. Not a stranger at all, not any more. Rick . . .

He got out of the car, walking around the front of it to stand easily recognisable in the car lights. 'My God, it is you,' he scowled. 'What the hell are you doing now?'

What an auspicious beginning! 'Getting wet!' she snapped at him, rain dripping off the end of her nose.

He gave an impatient sigh. 'You'd better get in, before we both drown. One of us is bad enough,' he muttered as he helped her into the warm comfort of the Jaguar.

She knew she looked like a drowned rat, she didn't need him to tell her that. Her hair was slicked to her scalp, the excess water now dripping down her neck. Not that her clothes could be any wetter, her raincoat had long ago stopped being waterproof, being only what they called 'water-resistant', which meant it kept the rain off you for about two minutes!

But Rick didn't have to make her quite so aware of how awful she must look. Resentment at once flared within her. 'I hardly chose to get wet,' she told him in a stilted voice. 'If you're worried about your leather car-seats getting wet——'

'I'm not,' he cut in grimly. 'If I were I wouldn't have stopped in the first place.'

'Thanks!'

'What did you expect? Sympathy?' He shook his head in disgust. 'It must have been obvious before you left Ampthull that the sky was going to open up.'

It had been a bit dark for this time of evening, but

she had been in such a rush to get home, to perhaps be able to go and visit this hateful man, that she hadn't really taken that much notice of the impending rain or its consequences.

'Well?' he barked as she made no comment.

Robyn sighed. 'Okay, so I realised it was going to rain, but I left anyway. I could hardly spend the night in Ampthull.'

'What happened to the bicycle?'

She explained why she couldn't use it. 'Although I would have got just as wet if I had,' she added moodily.

'Maybe,' he nodded. 'Although you would probably have been home by now.' He reached into his denims pocket. 'Here,' he held something out to her.

Expecting to see a handkerchief, she was surprised when she realised it was two ten-pound notes. She frowned. 'What's that?'

'For the new wheel you should have bought in the first place,' he said dryly, his face harsh in the gloom of the car.

'No, thank you,' she told him indignantly.

'Take it!' Rick ordered tightly.

'I said no!'

He gave her an impatient glare. 'You argue about everything!'

'And you're too damned bossy!'

Their mutual anger could clearly be felt in the tense silence in the car. Robyn shot Rick the occasional resentful glance, but facing only his rigid profile. Arrogant, overbearing creature!

'What happened to you last night?' he suddenly rapped out.

Robyn blinked, startled by the suddenness of the question. 'Last night?' she repeated.

'Yes,' he rasped. 'Your mother said you would come round to the house.'

She frowned. That she hadn't gone seemed to have greatly annoyed him. But why? She hadn't been to see him for weeks, and it didn't seem to have bothered him before then.

'I believe my mother said I might come round,' she said slowly, watching the angry tightening of his jaw, the cleft in his chin all the more noticeable.

'If you had time,' he finished grimly.

Robyn shrugged. 'Well, obviously I didn't have time.' Her tone was deliberately casual as she kept to her decision to play it cool.

'Obviously,' his mouth twisted. 'Who was he?'

'He?' He couldn't actually be jealous because he thought she had been out with another man last night, someone she preferred to him? She certainly hoped that was the reason for his strange attitude.

'The man you spent the evening with,' he said tightly.

He *had* to be jealous, surely there could be no other explanation. 'I spent the evening quietly at home with my family,' she told him softly.

Rick's mouth thinned. 'I see.'

'I didn't realise it was a firm promise,' she rubbed salt into the wound, enjoying his anger.

'It wasn't,' he snapped.

'Then I'm sure you weren't too disappointed,' she said sweetly.

'Not at all.' His tone was terse as he brought the car to a halt outside her home.

Robyn bit her lip as Rick turned in his seat, obviously waiting for her to get out. And she didn't want to, not now. 'I—I could always come back with you for a while now,' she offered tentatively.

He eyed her mockingly. 'Like that?' he taunted.

She put up a selfconscious hand to her wet hair, having momentarily forgotten her bedraggled appearance. She flushed. 'After I've changed.'

'I think not,' Rick shook his head. 'Not tonight. I'm busy.'

She went pale at his rejection. 'Who is she?' she returned his question of a few minutes ago.

He relaxed back in his seat, completely at ease. '*She* is a typewriter, the one you saw in my bedroom.'

His reference to his bedroom reminded her all' too vividly of the painful scene that had taken place there. And she had the feeling that Rick knew just how embarrassing she found the memory.

'What are you doing on it?' she asked waspishly.

'Typing,' he supplied dryly.

Robyn flushed. 'If you don't want to tell me then just say so,' she snapped.

'All right,' he sighed, his grey eyes calmly meeting the fire in her violet ones. 'I don't want to tell you,' he added curtly.

'Oh.'

'Satisfied?' he drawled.

She would never be that, not while she continued to be taunted by this man. He would reveal nothing of himself he didn't want to, making a mystery of his life both before he came here and now. And she wanted to know the answer to that mystery, although she doubted he would ever tell it to her.

'I think you should get indoors and out of that wet clothing,' he said at her continued silence. 'Take a bath and have a hot drink,' he advised.

'I——'

'Don't argue, Robyn,' he interrupted impatiently. 'You know I'm right.'

'According to you you always are,' she glared at him. 'Will you also be having a bath and a hot drink?'

'I didn't get as wet as you.'

He might only have been standing out in the rain a

matter of a few seconds, but like most summer storms the rain was absolutely pouring down, and Rick's shirt clung to his powerful chest and tapered waist, and even his denims were damp.

'I still think——'

'Okay, I'll have a drink,' he cut in abruptly.

'But not tea or coffee,' she guessed.

His mouth twisted. 'I doubt it.'

Robyn bit her bottom lip, knowing she couldn't delay getting out of the car any longer. 'Do you want me to come over tomorrow after work?'

He shrugged. 'Please yourself.'

Pain constricted her throat at his complete uninterest in seeing her again. 'Do *you* want me to?' she persisted.

'Like I said, please yourself.'

Her eyes flashed, her hands clenching at her sides as she fought down the urge to hit him. 'God, I hate you!' she choked.

Rick's mouth tightened. 'I'm not too keen on you either.'

She paled once again. 'That wasn't very nice.'

He sighed, pushing the damp swathe of his dark hair from his forehead. 'You certainly don't bring out the best in me,' he admitted. 'For instance, right now I——' he broke off. 'Never mind,' he dismissed grimly, and turned away, his jaw rigid.

Robyn sat forward, her expression one of eagerness. 'Right now . . .?' she prompted.

'It doesn't matter,' he said tersely, his profile stern.

'Rick, please!'

'All right!' His tone was savage as he turned fiercely to face her, grasping her arms painfully between his fingers. 'You asked for this!' His eyes glittered triumphantly before his head bent and his lips claimed hers.

His possession of her was complete, enfolding her roughly against his chest, bending her back over his arm to plunder her mouth with a passion that was instantaneous.

Robyn kissed him right back, uncaring that his roughness was bruising her, that her lips already ached from the contact, that Rick allowed no respite for her inexperience. She didn't feel inexperienced at that moment, arching against him as their bodies fused together in mutual longing.

Suddenly he thrust her away from him, his mouth twisting contemptuously. 'Why don't you stay away from me?' he rasped furiously. 'Haven't you learnt yet that where you're concerned I'm dangerous?'

She swallowed hard, still dazed from his kisses. 'Dangerous . . .?'

'Yes!' Rick turned away, his face harsh. 'God knows why, but I want you.' He looked at her with agonised eyes. 'And I don't want to take you.'

Robyn bit her lip, her eyes wide with bewilderment. 'Why not?' she asked quietly, her senses still alive from his fierce onslaught.

'You know damned well why not!' he explained.

'Tell me.'

He drew a ragged breath. 'When I take a woman to my bed I want exactly that—a woman.' He looked her over insultingly. 'Maybe in a couple of years you might qualify.'

She closed her eyes so that he shouldn't see the pain he was deliberately inflicting. 'There has to be a first time for everyone,' she choked, looking at him pleadingly.

He turned to flick the key in the ignition. 'Yours isn't going to be with me,' he dismissed abruptly.

'But you want me, you said you did!' Her desperation was unhidden, her love for this man glowing in her deeply violet eyes if he would just turn and look at her.

She had half guessed at the emotion the last time she

had been with him at the house, but now she knew it to be fact. She had fallen in love with a man she hardly knew, a man who made no secret of the fact that he didn't love her in return. But he wanted her! Surely most relationships started off with wanting first? She had felt that quicksilver emotion the first time she had seen him, had been physically attracted to his lithe body and dark good looks from that moment. Maybe it had taken him a little longer to feel the same way, but he wanted her now.

Rick's expression was grim. 'I'd want any attractive willing female at the moment. I told you, my sex drive is higher than most, and I've been here seven weeks already.'

'You mean you——' she licked her suddenly dry lips. 'You just want me because I'm here and—and willing?'

His mouth twisted, his appraisal insulting. 'You are, aren't you?'

'I was,' she corrected quietly, suddenly feeling numb.

Rick looked straight ahead, revving up the engine of the car as if impatient to be gone. 'Goodbye, Robyn,' his tone was almost gentle. 'You'll thank me for this one day.'

'I wouldn't count on it,' she choked.

His hand moved to cover one of hers as it rested on her thigh. 'You will,' he assured her.

'Rick, I——'

'Goodbye, Robyn,' he repeated pointedly.

Her bottom lip trembled. 'You aren't leaving?'

'No, you are. Out you get.'

'I meant leaving Sanford.'

'No, I'm not leaving, not yet. But don't come to Orchard House any more, not if you have any sense at all.'

She gave a wan smile. 'I don't.'

He shrugged. 'Then I won't let you in.'

Robyn knew he meant it, it was there in the determination of his mouth, the coldness of his icy grey eyes. 'You'll say goodbye before you do—finally leave?' she quavered.

He gave an abrupt nod. 'I'll say goodbye. Now, are you going to get out or do I have to physically push you?'

Any contact with him would be better than nothing, but she knew he wouldn't thank her for forcing him to touch her again. 'I'm going,' she said huskily, pushing open the car door.

She had no sooner stepped on to the pavement than the Jaguar accelerated away. The car belonged to a wealthy man, and yet the untidiness of Rick's clothing pointed to him being the opposite of that. Not that it mattered to her what he was, she loved him anyway.

For the first time in her young life she was in love, and it had to be with a man she just couldn't have. She might not know much about Rick, but she did know he had no intention of marrying anyone as young and inexperienced as she was.

And so much for her coolness! She had caught fire as soon as he touched her, was still burning from the contact. And he had known exactly how vulnerable she was towards him, had known and yet still rejected her. But this time she felt no shame, knew that if he ever changed his mind about her she would go to him willingly.

Her father was just closing up when she entered the shop, although he looked up from his book-work to smile at her. The incident that had so upset her had been forgotten by them, and Robyn realised that her father was just being his protective self. It was only because it had been about Rick that she had been so sensitive to the remark; normally she would have laughed off such an idea.

'Is it raining?' her father frowned at her wet appearance.

'Oh, Dad!' she giggled at his vague expression. 'Of course it's raining.'

'I didn't realise. Well, you'd better go upstairs and change. Your mother has your dinner ready.'

She was ushered upstairs to bath and change before her mother would even consider serving her meal. She also washed her hair, leaving it to dry as she ate her food.

'Was that Mr Howarth's car I saw outside?' her mother asked casually.

Robyn blushed. Her mother wasn't a nosey person, she didn't have time to be, and yet somehow she never seemed to miss anything. 'It was,' she acknowledged quietly.

'Will you be going over later?'

'No.'

'Oh?'

'No,' she said abruptly, not at all anxious to tell her mother that she and Rick had had yet another argument. Besides, it hadn't exactly been an argument, more a desire on Rick's part to let her know where she stood with him. And he had made his feelings more than clear.

'Have you two fallen out again?' her mother sighed her exasperation.

Robyn's mouth quirked into a smile. 'You make us sound like a couple of children!'

'You seem to act that way when you're together. Ordinarily Mr Howarth seems to be a very nice man, very levelheaded, and yet you and he seem to do nothing but argue. And I know it can't be all your fault, you have a temper, but it usually needs to be kindled. Mr Howarth obviously does that all too easily.'

She gave a rueful smile. 'I seem to do the same thing to him.'

'I've noticed,' her mother said dryly. 'And so have other people. Mrs Reed was in today trying to get information out of me about the two of you.'

'Goodness, she's an old gossip,' Robyn said moodily.

'She doesn't have any excitement of her own, so she tries to get it second-hand. Needless to say I didn't tell her anything.'

Knowing how relentlessly the other woman plied her questions, Robyn thought her mother probably deserved a medal for withstanding her. 'Thanks, Mum,' she grinned.

'I really think——'

Billy burst into the room, the bag that he had used to deliver his evening newspapers still slung over his shoulder, his hair as wet as Robyn's had been when she got home.

'Hey, guess what?' he cried.

'We don't need to guess anything,' his mother said dryly. 'I'm sure you're going to tell us anyway.'

He threw the bag down in an armchair, uncaring of its wet state. 'Do you know why I'm so late?'

'Tell us,' his mother invited patiently.

'Well, I couldn't believe it when I saw the car. It was such a mess, all crumpled in at the front, although the engine was still going, surprisingly enough. Of course I switched it off, but——'

'Billy,' his mother was sitting forward now, her face deadly serious, 'what are you talking about?'

'It was such a fantastic car too,' he shook his head.

'Billy!'

He blinked. 'Sorry. I was just—It all happened so suddenly, I've only just had time to think about it. I had to ring for an ambulance, you see, and—Well, I suppose I'm a bit shaken up.'

Considering what a tough little boy he was this must have taken some courage to admit. 'Just tell us slowly,

Billy,' Robyn suggested gently. 'Someone had an accident, right?'

'Mm,' he nodded, sitting down abruptly. 'Mr Howarth was slumped over the wheel of the car——'

'Mr Howarth?' She went deathly pale. '*Rick* had an accident?' Her voice was shrill in her distress.

'Yes,' Billy nodded. 'His car was wrapped around a tree, and——'

Robyn didn't hear any more. The world suddenly went black as she fainted.

CHAPTER FIVE

SHE couldn't have been unconscious long, but it was long enough for her mother to have called her father in from the shop, and for him to have lifted her still form on to the sofa. She was propped up against some cushions when she came out of her faint.

'Rick,' she mumbled weakly. 'Rick!' She shot up into a sitting position, her eyes fevered.

'It's all right, Robyn,' her mother soothed. 'Dad's going to drive you into Ampthull.'

He looked startled. 'I am?'

'You are,' he was told firmly.

'Okay,' he shrugged defeat, 'I am.'

Robyn stood up, swaying slightly. 'Can we go now?' Rick had been injured, how badly she just didn't know, he could even be dead, and she had to get to the hospital as soon as possible. God, if he were dead . . .

She went white at the thought of it, and her mother was instantly at her side. 'I think you should leave it for a few minutes,' she advised softly. 'Give yourself chance to get over the shock.'

Robyn's face was raw with pain, her eyes shadowed. 'No, I—I have to go now,' she insisted dazedly. Rick couldn't be dead, he couldn't be! Tears flooded her eyes and she began to sob.

'It's the shock.' Her mother instantly pushed her into a chair. 'Now you stay there while I get you a hot drink. Your father will telephone the hospital while I get you a cup of tea.'

'I will?' he sounded doubtful.

'Would you, Dad?' Robyn looked at him pleadingly.

His expression instantly softened. 'Of course I will, love, if you promise to drink your tea.'

'I promise,' she agreed eagerly, desperate to know how Rick was and yet terrified of telephoning the hospital herself. If they should say he was dead—God, she would want to die herself!

The tea was strong and sweet, exactly the way she hated it the most, but at least it pulled her together. She looked up eagerly as her father returned from making the telephone call.

'He's having X-rays now,' he told her as she stood up. 'So they don't know the extent of his injuries yet.'

A sigh of relief left her body. 'At least he's alive!'

'Of course he is,' Billy spoke for the first time since Robyn had fainted. 'I could have told you that,' he added scornfully.

'Then why didn't you?' his mother scolded, fluttering worriedly about Robyn as she pulled her jacket on in preparation for leaving for the hospital. 'You could have saved Robyn all this worry.'

Billy shrugged. 'No one asked me.'

'Well, we're asking now,' Robyn said angrily. 'What exactly happened after you found—found Rick in his car?'

'He got out of the car before the ambulance arrived. He was a bit shaky, but still on his feet.'

She began to shake with reaction. 'I wish you had told me that earlier. I've been imagining all sorts of things!'

Her brother seemed puzzled by her behaviour. 'What sort of things?' he frowned.

'Oh, Billy,' she shook her head, 'you'll never know, you really won't.'

He gave a disgusted snort. 'If you ask me you're acting a bit strange. Mr Howarth——'

'Well, no one did ask you,' their mother gave him a push in the direction of the stairs. 'Go and have a bath, you're dripping water everywhere.'

'Oh, Mum,' he complained, 'I had a bath yesterday.'

'And now you can have another one,' she said unsympathetically.

'Spoilsport!' he muttered as he slowly dragged his feet up the stairs.

'Let's get going,' Robyn's father said briskly.

'You're sure you don't mind?' she asked anxiously.

'I——'

'Of course he doesn't mind,' her mother cut in warningly. 'I'll warm your supper through when you get back, Peter.'

'I can always get a taxi,' Robyn suggested, sure that her father wouldn't appreciate a warmed-through dinner.

'I won't hear of it this time of night,' her mother said firmly. 'Your father can take you. You can get a taxi back if it looks as if you're going to be some time.'

Robyn's father opened the door for her to exit. 'How your mother loves to organise!' He shook his head.

'And how lost you would be if I didn't!' and she followed them out of the room.

Robyn knew that her parents were talking in this joking manner to try and ease her tension, but right now she couldn't cope with anything else but the thought of Rick injured at the hospital.

The rain hadn't abated, making the driving conditions difficult and slow, which didn't help her impatience in the least. Her father was always a careful driver, but tonight he had to be particularly so.

'Shall I come in with you?' he asked as he parked the car at the Casualty Department of the hospital.

'Er—No, I—I think I'd rather go in alone.' She looked down awkwardly at her hand, knowing her parents must be puzzled by her behaviour. 'I've been making rather a fool of myself lately,' she shrugged uncomfortably. 'I'd rather you didn't see me do it again.'

His hand came out to cover both of hers. 'If you care

for the man, and you obviously do, then it isn't making a
fool of yourself. Just give him room to breathe, hmm?'

She gave a shaky smile. 'I thought you said you didn't
know him.'

'I know the type,' he squeezed her hand comfortingly.
'They need plenty of space.'

'I've noticed,' she grimaced, bending forward to kiss
him warmly on the cheek. 'I'll let you know what's happening as soon as I know myself.'

The Casualty Department was brightly lit, strangely
deserted of people, although perhaps not so strangely,
since it was almost seven o'clock in the evening. Still,
she had thought these places were always busy, always
a hive of activity.

'Can I help you?'

Robyn started, so deep in thought she hadn't noticed
the approach of the nurse now standing in front of her,
a middle-aged woman who looked as if she had something more important to do than spend time being polite
to a confused-looking teenager.

'I've come to see Mr Howarth,' she said breathlessly.

The woman frowned. 'Come to collect him, you
mean,' she corrected waspishly.

Robyn's face lit up with excitement. 'He's well enough
to go home?'

The nurse gave a disgusted sniff. 'That's a matter of
opinion. Are you a relative of his?'

Colour flooded her cheeks as she wished she could
say yes. 'No. I—I'm a friend.' She hoped she was still
that at least!

'I see.' The woman looked down her nose at her. 'In
that case perhaps you would like to sit outside in the
waiting-room. Mr Howarth should be out soon, the
doctor is just strapping him up.'

Robyn swallowed hard. 'Strapping him up . . .?'

The nurse gave an impatient sigh. 'It's the usual practice with broken ribs.'

'Rick has broken ribs?' she gasped. 'I mean—Mr Howarth has?'

'He does.'

'But—but surely he shouldn't be going home straight away?' Robyn protested. 'Shouldn't he be admitted for a few days?'

The nurse looked affronted. 'Of course he should,' she confirmed haughtily. 'That's already been explained to Mr Howarth, but other than actually tying him to the bed we can't force him to stay here.'

Robyn bit her lip. 'I see. Well, I——'

'Robyn!'

She turned to see Rick just leaving a room a few doors down the corridor. She ran towards him, just remembering in time not to throw herself into his arms. With broken ribs that was the last thing he needed!

She looked up at him shyly, noting how grey he looked, fine lines of strain etched beside his nose and mouth. He must be in extreme pain, and yet he stood ramrod-straight, his only other apparent injury a cut to his brow. 'Rick . . .' she said huskily, her violet-eyed gaze eating in the warm vitality of him. After what she had been imagining broken ribs seemed quite trivial—although she doubted Rick felt that way about them!

'What are you doing here!' he rasped, his eyes narrowed.

Not a very encouraging welcome, but she wasn't going to be put off now, not with that superior-looking nurse watching them as closely as she was.

She moved forward, reaching up on tiptoe to kiss him on the lips, taking care not to touch him and so cause him unnecessary pain, blushing at the mockery in his eyes as she moved away. She linked her arm through the crook of his with a challenging flick of her head.

'I've come to take you home,' she told him stubbornly, the look in her eyes daring him to dispute her right to do that.

His mouth twisted as he looked down at her, taking his time about answering, deliberately so, Robyn thought. 'That's good of you,' he drawled, making no effort to remove her hand from his arm. He looked up at the nurse. 'Thanks for your help,' he said with a sincerity that had been noticeably absent seconds earlier when he had spoken to Robyn. 'I appreciate it,' he added deeply.

'If you appreciate it that much,' a doctor appeared from the room behind Rick, 'why won't you let us admit you for a couple of days, just to make sure there are no complications?'

Rick gave a tolerant smile. 'I've already told you why. Besides,' he smiled down at Robyn, his eyes full of mockery, 'I couldn't possibly leave a beautiful girl like Robyn on her own too long. I'd lose her to someone else, someone younger.'

Robyn stiffened at his taunting smile, would have removed her hand from his arm if his fingers hadn't clamped around hers to stop her. 'Shall we go, darling?' she enquired sweetly, getting back at him that way. Two could play at this game. 'I'm sure these good people have more—important things to do.'

He raised his eyebrows. 'That's putting me firmly in my place.'

'No,' she said innocently. 'If you were in your place you would be in a hospital bed. It's pure madness——'

'Thank you, Robyn,' he interrupted coldly. 'I'll take your criticism as said.'

She blushed at his anger. 'If you're ready to leave . . .?'

He nodded. 'I'm ready.' He made his goodbyes to the doctor and nurse, his hand firm on Robyn's elbow as he guided her outside. Once outside he immediately removed his hand. 'Now what's the reason behind you're being here?' he rasped.

'I already told you, I'm here to take you home, or rather, my father is. He's parked over here.' She walked in the direction of her father's car.

'Wait a minute!' Rick caught hold of her arm, spinning her round, wincing with pain as it jarred his broken ribs. 'You mean,' his eyes narrowed, 'that you dragged your father out this time of night to pick up a complete stranger?'

'You aren't a stranger to me!'

'But your father——'

'Unless you've forgotten, it was Billy who found you. It's only natural that we should all be concerned about you.' Her voice was stilted at his ingratitude.

'Is that the only reason?'

Her eyes snapped with anger. 'You're damned arrogant if you think I came here for any other reason! I wouldn't cross the road to help you if you were——' Her words were cut off by the fierce pressure of his lips on hers.

'Hell!' he swore, flinching back as the movement caused agonising pain to shoot through his body. 'Damn, damn, damn!' He doubled over with the agony of it.

'Rick?' Her anger at once faded to be replaced by anxious concern. 'Oh, Rick, are you all right?'

'Fine,' he choked. 'Except that I feel as if I'm dying,' he added derisively.

'You——'

'Let's get him to the car.' Miraculously her father had appeared at her side, helping Rick walk over and get into the car. 'You sit in the back, Robyn,' he instructed.

She scrambled inside, still watching Rick as he sat completely straight in the front sea. 'Let's get Rick home and into bed,' she told her father. 'Which, incidentally, is where he should be right now.'

'I already gathered that,' her father said dryly. 'Hang on, Mr Howarth, this could be a bumpy ride.'

'I'll manage,' Rick mumbled, obviously not 'managing' at all.

Each little bump and pothole in the road seemed larger than life to Robyn, and she felt sure they must to Rick too, although he didn't complain. In fact he was so quiet she began to wonder if he could possibly have passed out. Then she heard him groan as her father swerved to avoid a particularly large hole in the road.

'Sorry, son,' her father said softly.

'It's okay,' Rick grimaced.

It felt strange to Robyn to hear her father call Rick 'son'; there really couldn't be much difference in their ages, her father only being in his mid-forties to Rick's thirty-six.

They finally reached Orchard House, although the journey seemed to have taken forever, even longer than the journey to the hospital. Rick got out of the car with an effort, and her father helped him inside the house.

'I'll be fine now,' Rick assured them.

She didn't think he would be any such thing. He was grey now, his breath coming in painful rasps. 'I'm staying,' she said firmly. 'You go on home, Dad, Mum will be worried. I'll just help Rick to bed and then come home myself.'

'I can help you here first,' her father insisted.

'I'd really rather be alone,' Rick groaned. 'I thank you both for your help, but I want to be on my own now.' He turned on his heel and walked up the stairs.

'Dad——'

'I know, love,' he squeezed her hand understandingly. 'Your mother and I will expect you when we see you.'

Robyn gave a tremulous smile. 'Thank you, Dad,' and she kissed him gratefully.

By the time she got up the stairs Rick had managed

to half struggle out of his jacket, although he looked as if every movement was now causing him pain. His expression was bleak, his eyes almost black as he looked up and saw her. 'I thought I told you to leave,' he growled.

'You did.' She slipped his jacket off his other arm, beginning to unbutton his shirt as he relaxed back on the bed with a sigh. 'Aren't you glad I don't take any notice of you?' she teased, hoping he didn't notice the way her hands shook as she smoothed the shirt off his powerful shoulders, a thick white bandage around his chest to support his broken ribs.

'This time I am.' His eyes were closed in exhaustion. 'Well, don't stop now,' he said sleepily. 'I always sleep in the raw.'

The next few minutes were the most embarrassing of Robyn's young life. She had never seen a man naked before, let alone stripped one, although Rick's closed eyes made it easier for her. The reason his eyes were closed soon became apparent; he was fast asleep.

She pulled the bedclothes up over him, glad that he could at least rest. He looked younger in sleep, all mockery and derision erased. He looked more handsome too, if that were possible. Her breath caught in her throat as she stood looking down at him, wishing she had the right to share that bed with him, to enjoy the power of his magnificent body.

He was beautiful to look at, wonderfully strong and powerfully muscled, his strength still there even though he was asleep. When he was awake he was dangerous. Hadn't he already warned her of that!

But right now she had to decide what to do about the night ahead. 'We'll expect you when we see you,' her father had said, but she doubted he would expect that to be tomorrow morning. But she could hardly leave Rick on his own when he was ill, she doubted he would even be able to get out of bed, let alone anything else.

There was a telephone down in the hall, so she called home, slightly relieved when her mother answered the telephone; she doubted if her father would be sympathetic to her decision to spend the night here. She was right; she could hear him protesting in the background as her mother told her that of course she couldn't leave Mr Howarth alone, and that they would see her some time tomorrow. Robyn very wisely rang off before her father could come on the line and voice his objections personally.

She had no choice but to spend the night in the bedroom with Rick, the absence of furniture in the rest of the house making this the only room in which she could be relatively comfortable; at least there was an armchair in here, even if it was lumpy and hard.

Rick seemed to be in a deep sleep, probably due to the painkilling drugs they had given him at the hospital. They must have given him something to ease the pain; she couldn't believe he would refuse even that much help.

If only her own night could be spent as comfortably as his seemed to be; the chair was not only lumpy but also too small to sleep in. If she sat up straight her head fell to one side and woke her up, and if she slumped down in the chair enough to rest her head on the back, then she tended to slide completely out of the chair and on to the ground. She seriously contemplated sharing the bed with Rick—after all, broken ribs must make him incapable—but she didn't think she could bear his derision in the morning.

And so she sat up straight in the chair, unable to sleep, but the fact that the light was off preventing her doing anything else instead, like reading. Each minute seemed like an hour, and as Rick continued to sleep she began to think her presence here was unnecessary after all.

Then some time after four Rick rolled over on to his side, his groan of pain bringing him awake. Robyn was instantly alert, moving to the bedside.

Rick's eyes registered his surprise as he blinked to clear his head, his lashes long and thick. 'What time is it?' he demanded gruffly, obviously deciding that it wasn't so strange to see her in his bedroom after all.

'About quarter past four,' she answered softly.

His eyes widened. 'In the morning?'

Robyn nodded confirmation. 'How do you feel now?'

'Bloody awful,' he growled, struggling to sit up. 'And don't tell me I should have stayed in hospital,' he said warningly.

'I wasn't going to,' she told him indignantly. 'Although I find it slightly strange that a grown man should be afraid——'

'I'm not afraid, damn you!' he cut in furiously. 'I just don't consider myself sick enough to take up space in a hospital bed.'

'I know of a few people who disagree with you.'

His expression darkened even more. 'What the hell do they know? Are you going to help me up or just stand there and watch me struggle?' he said nastily, pushing back the confining bedclothes.

Robyn gulped; his body was a shadowy form in the darkness. But she could still recall undressing him, and the intimacy of the situation washed over her.

'I don't think you should make any unnecessary moves,' she advised hastily, wishing she could dispel her awareness of this man, and knowing she would never be able to do that, not while she still had breath in her body.

His mouth twisted mockingly. 'I don't think this move is unnecessary, Robyn,' he taunted.

'Oh!' She blushed fiery red.

Rick chuckled, then his humour turned to a wince. 'Don't make me laugh,' he groaned. 'God, now I know what's meant by the saying, "It only hurts when I laugh"!

Help me up, will you, Robyn.' He held out a hand.

'Of course.' She squashed down her feelings of embarrassment and put her arm about his waist, trembling as she touched his warm vibrant flesh. 'I'm sorry,' she mumbled, biting her lip painfully.

'I'm hardly in any condition to suddenly leap on you,' he derided.

Robyn looked up. 'I wouldn't mind if you did,' she revealed huskily, past hiding her emotions where this man was concerned. She had almost lost him tonight, and she would rather be her usual truthful self anyway, it came more naturally to her.

'Robyn——'

'Rick, please——'

'No!' His voice was harsh. 'You're taking advantage of a sick man,' he added scornfully.

She swallowed hard. 'I'm sorry. I—I'll save it for when you're well again.'

'I wish you wouldn't,' he said cruelly, his face harsh.

'Well, I'm going to,' she insisted stubbornly.

He shrugged. 'You'll only get hurt.'

'So I'll get hurt,' Robyn choked.

'Don't say I didn't warn you,' he snapped. He stopped outside the bathroom door. 'I think I can manage from here,' he taunted. 'I'll give you a call when I'm ready to go back to bed.'

Robyn went back into the bedroom to wait for him, knowing that he meant his warning. She might love him, and she thought that he was now aware of it, even though it hadn't verbally been admitted, but she couldn't force him to love her in return. And he didn't love her, he was making that clear to her.

'Robyn . . .'

She turned, tears glistening in her violet-blue eyes. 'Yes?' she quivered, fighting back those tears from actually cascading down her cheeks.

For a moment Rick looked angry, whether with himself or her she couldn't have said. Then he leant heavily against the doorframe. 'Help me back,' he requested huskily.

'Of course!' She was instantly contrite for her thoughtlessness, all embarrassment at his nakedness now gone, mainly because he was unembarrassed himself.

He leant heavily against her as he made his way slowly over to the bed, having used up most of his strength getting from the bathroom to the bedroom door.

'Thanks,' he sighed his relief as he lowered himself gingerly down on to the bed. 'You're a good kid,' he looked up at her gratefully.

'Don't!' Her eyes darkened with pain.

His mouth set in a firm line. 'Don't what?'

'Don't try and reduce me to the level of a child!' she said tautly. 'I may not be as old as you——'

'You certainly aren't!'

'But I'm not a child either,' she continued fiercely, her hands clenched at her sides. 'I'm a woman, with a woman's feelings and emotions, and I—I love you.' She froze with the enormity of her admission.

'Robyn——'

'No, don't feel sorry for me!' She turned away from the sympathy in his face, the pity. 'I'll go now,' she said jerkily. 'It's almost morning anyway. I—I have to get a couple of hours' sleep before I go to work. Will you be all right if I leave now?' She still couldn't look at him, her back rigid with the effort it cost her not to break down and cry.

'Yes, I'll be fine. But——'

'Good,' she interrupted briskly, picking up her jacket. 'I—Someone will be over later to see if you're all right.' But not her, not her! She couldn't face him again, not after what she had just done. She ran to the door.

VISIT 4 MAGIC PLACES FREE!

Time of the Temptress by Violet Winspear
Trapped in the jungles of Africa, Eve's only chance for survival was total dependence on the mercenary Major Wade O'Mara. He had the power to decide her fate. But only she could make him give in to desire.

Say Hello to Yesterday by Sally Wentworth
Seeing Nick after seven years made Holly realize it was her parents who ruined their marriage. Now that she had found him, she knew that their love had never died. And she was determined to make him love her again.

Born Out of Love by Anne Mather
Charlotte had paid for one night's pleasure with years of pain and loneliness. Ten years after Logan had deserted her and the baby, they met unexpectedly on San Cristobal... where their love affair seemed destined to begin again.

Man's World by Charlotte Lamb
She had everything going for her. Brains. Beauty. And a sterling wit. Her only problem was men. She hated them. That is, until Eliot decided to make her see otherwise.

Love surrounds you in the pages of Harlequin Romances

Harlequin Presents romance novels are the ultimate in romantic fiction . . . the kind of stories that you can't put down . . . that take you to romantic places in search of adventure and intrigue. They are stories full of the emotions of love . . . full of the hidden turmoil beneath even the most innocent-seeming relationships. Desperate clinging love, emotional conflict, bold lovers, destructive jealousies and romantic imprisonment—you'll find it all in the passionate pages of **Harlequin Presents** romance novels.

Let your imagination roam to the far ends of the earth. Meet true-to-life people. Become intimate with those who live larger than life.

Harlequin Presents romance novels are the kind of books you just can't put down . . . the kind of experiences that remain in your dreams long after you've read about them.

Let your imagination roam to romantic places when you...

'Robyn, for God's sake!' Rick was struggling to sit up. 'Robyn, don't go like this.'

'I have to!' The tears were falling unheeded now. 'I love you, and I'm not ashamed of it, but surely you can see I can't stay here now?'

Only his laboured breathing broke the lengthy silence. 'If you aren't ashamed of loving me,' he said softly, his eyes a mesmerising grey as he held out his hand to her, 'then come here.'

She licked her suddenly dry lips, her expression wary. 'C-Come there?'

'Yes,' he confirmed tautly. 'Come here so that I can touch you.'

Robyn swallowed hard. 'Do—do you want to?'

'God, yes!' he groaned achingly.

She didn't hesitate any longer, but dropped her jacket and ran to him, remembering his cracked ribs at the last moment. 'Oh, Rick!' She looked down at him with glowing eyes, longing to go to him, but afraid of hurting him.

His hand was gentle on her wrist, pulling her down on to the bed beside him. 'I can only keep saying no for so long. Just don't expect this to be the experience of a lifetime, I'm more than a little incapacitated at the moment,' he grimaced.

She felt no fear, no reservation about giving herself completely to this man, and yet she was concerned for him. After all, it was only a few hours since he had been injured in the accident. 'We can wait,' she said huskily, giving him a shy smile, 'until you're better.'

'You might be able to,' his hand was fevered in her blonde hair, 'but I can't wait a second longer. I've denied myself you for too long now. I have to have you *now*, Robyn,' he said fiercely, tugging her down into a lying position beneath him, his mouth possessively covering hers.

Robyn kissed him back, holding nothing back from him, sighing her pleasure as he slowly unbuttoned her shirt, her bra no barrier to his questing fingers, her breasts swelling into his cupping hand.

'God, you're so desirable,' he moaned, moving his mouth slowly down her body to claim one rose-tinted nipple between his arousing lips.

She trembled against him, pleasure so nerve-shattering shooting through her body that for a moment she thought she was going to faint. Rick seemed to sense that he was going too fast for her, and returned his mouth to hers.

'Gently,' he groaned against her lips, his tongue coming out to run caressingly along her lower lip, his hand now still at her breast although he held her possessively. 'Although God knows I don't feel like being gentle!' He kissed her again, his mouth drugging against hers, moving slowly against her, taking her along on a tide of sensual abandon.

When his hand moved to the fastening of her skirt Robyn raised no objections, but helped him remove the last of her clothing, looking up at him shyly as he sat back to gaze at every naked inch of her.

His jaw tightened, passion blazing darkly in his eyes. 'Lord, but you're lovely!' he breathed raggedly. 'Are you sure you want to go through with this?'

'Don't you?'

'Hell, yes,' he said dismissively. 'But I don't want there to be any regrets on your part.'

She looked up at him unflinchingly. 'I don't regret, and I won't regret, one moment of being with you,' she told him with quiet certainty.

He buried his face in her throat. 'That was your last chance to escape, there won't be another.'

Their caresses were fevered now, their desire becoming unbearable, until only complete possession would satisfy both of them. Robyn's nails dug pleasurably into Rick's taut back, the hair on his chest abrasive to her tender breasts, causing a mad excitement to course through her veins.

'Oh God!' Rick gasped suddenly, and moved away from her, his body hunched over, his face white.

Robyn scrambled on to her knees, desire forgotten in her concern for the man she loved. 'What's the matter?' she demanded anxiously. 'What happened?'

'It's my ribs.' He swore under his breath. 'I think we're going to have to wait after all, little one,' he added ruefully.

'How stupid I am!' she instantly blamed herself. 'Lie back, Rick—that's right,' she helped him into a prone position. 'We'll forget about—this, for now,' colour flooded her cheeks at the warmth that was still in his eyes as he gazed up at her. 'You should be resting, not—not——'

'Trying to seduce young girls,' he finished dryly.

Robyn zipped up her skirt and pulled on her shirt, feeling more relaxed now that she was dressed. 'It was hardly seduction,' she pointed out.

'No,' his mouth twisted, 'it didn't get that far.' His expression darkened. 'Luckily for you I collapsed before that happened.'

'It wasn't lucky at all,' she told him firmly. 'At least, not as far as I'm concerned.'

Rick closed his eyes, his face grey. 'I think you'd better go now. We can talk tomorrow—today, when you get back from work.'

Her eyes showed her disappointment with this arrangement. 'But I want to spend the day with you.'

'And I want to sleep,' he said wearily.

She bit her lip. 'You don't want me around, right?'

'How clever of you to guess!' His eyes flickered open at her gasp. 'Leave it for now, Robyn. I'm in pain at the

moment and you happen to be the only person here I
can take it out on.' He grimaced. 'Frustration doesn't
help.'

'No . . .' She blushed. 'All right, I—I'll come back
tonight.' She moved to the door.

'Hey, Robyn!' His soft caressing voice reached out to
her.

'Yes!' She turned almost eagerly.

He held out his hand to her. 'Don't would-be seducers
merit a goodbye kiss?' he teased.

'Oh yes,' she smiled tremulously, her eyes glowing as
she ran to him, going down on her knees beside the bed.
She bent and kissed him softly on the lips. 'I love you,
Rick,' she told him huskily.

His breath caught in his throat. 'I don't think I've
ever met anyone like you before,' he smoothed the hair
at her temple. 'Your honesty and complete lack of guile
disarm me in a way I find unnerving.'

He made it sound as if this rarely, if ever, happened
to him—and that he didn't like the feeling. 'Poor Rick,'
she laughed softly.

A look of irritation crossed his face, to be slowly
replaced by a rueful smile. 'I can see I'll have to watch
you, you're the type that likes to twist a man up in
knots.'

'Not you, Rick,' she chuckled. 'Never you.'

'Let's hope not,' he growled. 'Off you go, Robyn,
before I change my mind and decide to try and seduce
you again. And don't say you wouldn't mind,' he cut in
before she could speak. 'I would. I don't think your
initiation into lovemaking should be with someone
who's in agony before he begins.'

'I never said it would be my initiation,' she told him
indignantly, trying desperately to remember what she
had told him.

'You didn't need to. For someone who said sex bored

them you respond in a most unbored manner.'

Robyn blushed. 'I can't help it——'

'No need to be ashamed of a perfectly normal response,' he said gently. 'I wasn't exactly "bored" myself, now was I?'

'No,' she grinned, knowing he had been as aroused as she had.

'Right. Now please go. I really do need to sleep.'

'Tonight——'

'Let's wait and see what tonight brings.' He kissed her hard on the lips, turning away in conclusion of the encounter.

Robyn felt as if she floated home on a cloud, not going to bed but making herself some breakfast and a pot of coffee, and she was still sitting in the kitchen when her mother came downstairs.

'What time did you get home?' she wanted to know.

'A couple of hours ago.'

'Did Mr Howarth manage to get any sleep?'

'A few hours.' Robyn blushed, getting up and moving to the door in case her mother should see her embarrassment and guess the reason for it. After last night, none of her family could be in any doubt about her feelings towards Rick, or the commitment to him those feelings gave her.

'Where are you going?' her mother frowned.

'To get ready for work,' she smiled. 'I can't be late again.'

'You're going to work, after being up all night?'

'Of course.' She smiled brightly. 'Don't worry, Mum, I feel great.'

'But——'

'I'll be fine, really I will.' She kissed her concerned mother on the cheek before going upstairs to wash and change.

The day passed in a haze for Robyn, not a tired one,

but a euphoric one. She hummed to herself while she
worked, beaming at anyone who looked at her, includ-
ing Selma, a Selma who was pleasantly surprised by the
change in her.

'Find yourself a new boy-friend?' she wanted to
know.

'No,' Robyn answered happily.

'Then what—You're back with Rick! Are you? Is that
it?' Selma was almost as excited as Robyn.

'Mm,' she nodded.

'Going to keep him this time?' Selma asked slyly.

Robyn laughed. 'I'm working on it.'

She didn't even bother to go home after work that
evening, anxious to be with Rick as soon as possible.
She could always call home from Rick's house.

She didn't knock on the door but went straight in,
knowing that he would either still be in bed or resting in
that lumpy chair, certainly in no condition to come
downstairs and open the door to her.

'Rick?' she called out his name so that she wouldn't
startle him when she appeared in his bedroom. He didn't
answer, so she knew he must be asleep again. Well, that
wouldn't do him any harm, and when he woke up she
would make him something light to eat. And later . . .

The sight that met her eyes as she let herself quietly
into the bedroom caused despair to shoot through her
body. The bed, chair, and table remained, but everything
else, every personal item had been removed. Rick had
gone, removed himself as suddenly as he had arrived!

CHAPTER SIX

HER first thought, rather hysterically, was that Rick hadn't said goodbye to her as he had promised he would. Then she remembered that he had said goodbye, he had teased her about kissing her would-be seducer goodbye. If she had known it was to be a final parting she would have refused!

Why had he gone like this? Why, when they loved each other? But they didn't! Oh, she had been so stupid. Rick hadn't said he loved her, he had only shown her that he wanted her. And she had deceived herself into thinking it was love because she had wanted him to be in love with her.

He had warned her she would be hurt, but the pain she was going through now was unbearable. Rick had opted out of her life, left her at a time when she had been at her happiest.

How long she stood there she never afterwards knew, but it was dark by the time she pulled herself together enough to drag herself back downstairs, switch off the lights and close the door to Orchard House for the last time. She would never come back here; just to look at it from the outside would be painful reminder enough of her impetuous love for Rick.

She hadn't cried—she couldn't. Inside she was numb, past pain, past feeling, the pain too deep-rooted to even hurt her. Rick hadn't just rejected her, he had walked out of her life for good.

Her mother was in the kitchen when Robyn let herself into the house. 'My God, you're all right!' she cried, grasping Robyn's arm to make sure she was really there and not just a figment of her imagination. 'Where have you been, Robyn?' Concern gave way to anger. 'Your father and I have been so worried!'

'I went to see Rick——'

'But he isn't there!'

'How do you know that?' Robyn asked sharply.

'He came into the shop——'

'Oh,' she said dully. 'No, he isn't there. He's gone.'

'Then where have you been all this time? It's hours since you left work,' her mother frowned.

'I know. I—I was thinking.' She just wanted to go to her room, to be left alone in her misery.

'All this time?' her mother persisted.

'Yes,' Robyn snapped.

Her mother sighed. 'All right, dear. I can see you're upset. Although what your father will say . . . He's out looking for you, you know.'

'I'm sorry,' her voice was emotionless. 'Tell him I'm sorry.'

'You can tell him yourself, love. He'll be back soon.'

'I'd like to go to bed—if you don't mind.'

'Robyn . . .'

She looked at her mother with lifeless eyes. 'Yes?'

'Last night. Did you——'

'No.' She gave a bitter smile, knowing that she couldn't take any credit for that.

'Oh!' Her mother's sigh was obviously one of relief. 'I'm sorry for asking, dear, but I——'

'It's all right, Mum, I understand. Is it okay if I go to my room now?'

'Yes, of course. Are you really all right, Robyn?'

She gave a bright smile, totally false. 'Really. He wasn't for me, I knew that from the start. I'll get over it,' she lied.

'Sure?'

'Yes. I—When Rick came in today,' she bit her lip

painfully, 'did he—did he mention me?'

Her mother shook her head regretfully. 'I'm afraid not, dear.'

'Oh well,' she shrugged to hide the sudden shaft of pain that shot through her, 'never mind. I'll see you in the morning.'

She didn't sleep, but she didn't cry either. She stared silently into the darkness for hour after hour, her mind a blank, her emotions numb. She had heard her father return home, had heard his raised voice and her mother's soothing one. She appeared to be successful, for Robyn heard no further argument from her father.

He made no comment during the following weeks either, in fact none of her family did. The only person who did was Selma.

'Lost him again, didn't you?' Selma sat down next to her in the staff-room, as for once Robyn was unable to avoid her.

She had been doing just that for the last two weeks, making sure she never had the same coffee or lunch-break as the other girl. Today she realised her luck had changed. 'I beg your pardon?' she said coldly.

Selma bit hungrily into her cheese roll. 'Whatever you did you didn't do it right.'

Robyn paled. 'Selma——'

'Sorry,' the other girl grinned. 'But believe me, no man is worth the agony you're going through.'

Robyn's mouth twisted. 'You should know.'

'Bitchy!' Selma accepted goodnaturedly. 'And maybe I should know. I knew the first time I saw your Rick that you were going to get hurt. Trampled all over your heart and didn't give a damn, did he?'

Robyn bit her lip, this being the first time anyone had so much as mentioned Rick's name in her presence. 'No,' she answered strongly, her head back proudly. 'He didn't give a damn.'

If he had he would have telephoned her, written, got in touch with her somehow, the idea that maybe he had been called away unexpectedly quickly dying as she heard nothing from him. It was almost as if he had never existed. Only her aching battered heart told her that wasn't so.

Feeling had returned with a vengeance a few days after Rick's departure, leaving her pale and drawn, her severe weight loss not really suiting her already slender body.

'No man is that good,' Selma said dismissively.

'That good . . .?' Robyn turned to the other girl.

'In bed.' She pursed her lips thoughtfully. 'Although he did look very experienced. Still, he isn't worth ruining your looks over.'

Ruining her looks? Was she really? Considering she had never thought of herself as being more than moderately pretty this came as something of a surprise to her. Still, she couldn't be so unattractive or Rick wouldn't have wanted her. Rick, Rick, Rick—damn the man!

'That's better,' Selma said with satisfaction.

Robyn blinked at her. 'What is?'

'At least you're angry now,' she grinned. 'Oh yes, you are, and it's better than the long face you've been walking around with lately. Goodness, I've lost lots of boyfriends, but I don't let that get to me. Admittedly Rick Howarth was something out of the ordinary, but it was because he was that you couldn't hope to hold him. I would just feel glad to have known him, and then move on to the next man.'

Robyn shook her head. 'You don't understand. I— I——'

'You loved him,' Selma finished with a smile. 'I've been in love dozens of times. It doesn't mean a thing. Look, how about coming to the disco with me tonight? I'll introduce you to someone new, someone who'll make you forget all about Rick Howarth.'

'No, thank you, Selma——'

'You can't keep moping, Robyn,' the other girl interrupted her refusal. 'Find someone new, you'll find Rick will soon fade from your mind.'

Never! His memory was engraved on her heart for ever, and no matter who came after him they would always be a poor second.

'Oh, I know what you're thinking,' Selma laughed. 'But you're wrong. Give it time, you'll forget what he even looks like.'

She didn't do that, but she did finally agree to accompany Selma on one of her evenings at the disco. She quite enjoyed herself, so much so that she went out with the other girl several times during the next few weeks. Selma flitted from boy to boy, never seriously involved with any of them.

Robyn herself was asked out several times, refusing every time, but often accepting invitations to dance. Her mother and father were a little concerned about her new friend, although once they had met Selma, an outspoken but likeable Selma, they relaxed a little. She might be a little giddy, very gullible where men were concerned, but she made no attempt to make Robyn the same.

And then one night Robyn met Brian. He asked her to dance, and because she instantly liked the look of him she willingly accepted. He was tall and dark, with warm grey-blue eyes, aged about twenty, with a sophisticated manner older than his years.

'I don't usually come to these places,' he told her as they danced together. 'My cousin persuaded me to come tonight,' he smiled down at her. 'I'm glad he did.'

Robyn shyly returned that smile. 'Where is your cousin?'

'Dancing with your friend.'

'Really?' She turned to see Selma dancing with a tall

fair-haired boy, winking at Robyn as she saw her looking their way. 'So I see,' she returned her attention to
Brian.

'Can I buy you a drink?' he offered when their dance
came to an end.

She looked at him uncertainly. He seemed nice
enough, was very good-looking, and besides, what harm
could he do her in here? 'I think I would like that,' she
accepted huskily.

'Good,' he smiled his pleasure, and took her upstairs
where the drinks were served. He saw her seated at a
table before going to the bar to get their drinks.

'I'm Robyn Castle,' she told him shyly once he was
seated opposite her in the booth.

'Brian Walker,' he smiled warmly. 'I'm here on holiday.'

'In Ampthull?'

He nodded, laughing at her surprise. 'I'm staying with
my aunt and uncle, and of course Paul. I've been sent
here to come to my senses. I've been accepted at drama
school,' he explained, 'but my parents want me to
become a doctor like my father and my two brothers.
I'm of the opinion that three doctors in one family is
enough,' he grimaced.

'It does sound like it,' she agreed sympathetically.

'Besides which I keel over just at the sight of blood!'

Robyn laughed at his woebegone expression. 'That
does sound like quite a serious disadvantage for a
doctor.'

Brian nodded. 'I would have thought so. But they
insist I'll grow out of it. I even persuaded a friend of
Dad's to talk them out of their plans for me. It didn't
work.'

'Probably because the best person to talk to them is
you.'

'I have, but they—Never mind,' he gave a rueful smile,

'I didn't intend boring you to death with my problems.'

It was nice to have someone else's problems to think about. She hadn't even given Rick a thought for the last hour since meeting Brian. 'I'm interested,' she assured him. 'When are you supposed to start drama school?'

'Next month. Let's not talk about me any more, tell me about you.'

'There isn't much to tell,' she shrugged.

His hand covered hers as it rested on the table. 'Tell me anyway.'

Her short life-history didn't take more than a few minutes to relate. With one exception her life had so far been uneventful.

Brian watched her closely. 'I get the feeling you're holding something back.'

'You're imagining it.' Her voice was brittle.

He slowly shook his head. 'No, I don't think so. Did he hurt you badly?'

'Did who—Yes,' she admitted with a sigh. 'Very badly.' Damn his perception!

'Swine!' Brian's tone was fierce.

Robyn gave a wan smile. 'You can't force someone to love you.'

'I don't see how he could *not* love you.'

'Well, he didn't,' she said dully. 'And I'd rather not talk about him.'

Brian grinned. 'Suits me—I don't like competition anyway. Let's go and have another dance.'

When he asked to see her again Robyn accepted. Selma was asked out by the cousin too, so they all went out for a drink together the next evening.

Selma soon dropped the cousin, declaring he was a snob, although Robyn continued to go out with Brian. He was fun to be with, good-looking, and most of all he seemed to genuinely like her. He kissed her goodnight with a reserved passion, never asking for more than that, and after Rick's demanding caresses it was nice to be able to relax with a man.

Orchard House remained empty; no other tenants moved in, either renting or buying. The house remained as a constant reminder of her stupidity, and her emotions remained aloof from Brian.

'I only want to kiss you properly,' he complained one evening after they had been to the cinema together and she had fought his passionate kisses.

'I'm sorry, Brian,' she blushed.

He turned in his car seat to stare sightlessly out of the front window. 'I don't feel as if I'm getting anywhere with you.'

Robyn stiffened. 'I didn't know you wanted to.'

He gave an impatient sigh. 'I don't mean physically, although goodness knows you're attractive enough. I'm half in love with you, Robyn, surely you've guessed that?'

Yes, she had, but because she liked him so much, enjoyed being with him, she had hoped he would never put those feelings into words.

'I've even told my mother and father about you,' he added.

'And I'm sure they don't approve.' She had learnt over the last few weeks that Brian's parents belonged to the highest social bracket, that his father wasn't just a doctor, but that he practised in Harley Street. No wonder they had been so dismayed by Brian's decision to take up acting! They must have been shocked to the core.

'They're coming down at the weekend to meet you,' he revealed eagerly.

Robyn frowned. 'To meet me? Why?' she asked suspiciously.

'Because—well, because I told them I'm serious about you. That I want to marry you.'

Her eyes deepened to violet in her alarm. 'Why on earth did you tell them something like that?' she demanded to know.

'Because it's the truth. Oh, I know we've only known each other two weeks——'

'Ten days,' she corrected tautly.

'Okay, ten days,' he said dismissively. 'But I'm in love with you. I—I want you to be my wife.'

'You're being ridiculous, Brian,' she snapped. 'No one falls in love in so short a time.' But she had! And her love for Rick had remained constant.

'I have,' Brian insisted heatedly. 'Please say you'll meet my parents, Robyn. They're looking forward to it.'

From what she had learnt about Mr and Mrs Walker their sole purpose in coming down here would be to warn her off their youngest son. 'I can't, Brian,' she refused. 'It's too soon to tell how either of us feels, and it wouldn't be fair to your parents to put them in such a position.'

For a moment he looked mutinous, then he smiled. 'If I can put them off this weekend will you promise to come and stay with us in London soon?' He gave her his most charming smile.

London! Rick was in London, she was sure of it. And yet her chances of accidentally meeting him there were about nil. Still, just to know he was in the same town would be something.

'I'm not promising anything, Brian,' she said slowly. 'But I'll think about it.'

'You really will?'

She smiled at his eagerness. 'I really will. But no more mention of love. It's too soon, Brian, much too soon.'

'I won't change my mind, you'll see.'

And he didn't seem to, telephoning her constantly once he had gone back to London, his holiday over.

Robyn missed him, missed his companionship and the way he could always make her laugh.

'Nice young man,' her mother remarked one night when Robyn came back from answering yet another call from Brian.

'Very nice,' she agreed noncommittally, knowing that her parents had been pleased about her blossoming friendship with Brian after all her moping for Rick.

'You don't sound too sure.' Her mother looked at her closely.

'Oh, I'm sure I like him.' She chewed her bottom lip. 'I'm just not sure I want him to be serious about me.'

'And is he?'

'He says he is,' Robyn sighed.

'How serious?'

'He wants me to go and stay with his parents this weekend.'

'I see.' Her mother pursed her lips thoughtfully. 'Do you want to go?'

'I—I don't know. I—You see, I'm still confused about Rick. I'm not sure what I feel any more.' Except that she still loved Rick with every fibre of her being. But she did like Brian, in a way she more than liked him. If only she had never met Rick . . .

'Maybe a weekend in London is just what you need to help you decide,' her mother surprised her by saying. 'If you see Brian in his home setting perhaps your feelings for him will become clearer.'

'You think so?' She still sounded uncertain.

'I think it's worth a try.'

Robyn grimaced. 'But isn't it a bit formal, meeting his parents?'

Her mother smiled. 'I don't see why—we've met Brian.'

'But it isn't the same.'

'Maybe not. But surely it can't do any harm. You're

only going to meet his parents, Robyn. I doubt he could arrange the wedding over the weekend.'

She gave a wan smile at her mother's teasing. Her parents had been worried about her, she knew that. And maybe a weekend in London would help to clear her mind of Rick. 'Do you think Dad will let me go?' He had become even more protective of her since her unhappy love for Rick.

'You just leave your father to me,' her mother said. 'Just make the arrangements with Brian, there won't be any objection from your father.'

And there wasn't. He even drove her to the station to catch the train to London. Brian had wanted to come and pick her up, but she had declined the offer, not seeing the point of him driving all the way down here just to drive back again.

But he did meet her at the station at the other end, and their kiss was one of mutual enthusiasm. Maybe she could learn to love Brian after all. It was only two months since Rick had left, maybe she just hadn't given herself time to get over him. She was certainly pleased to see Brian again anyway.

The Walker house was everything she had dreaded it being, from its exclusive setting to the many servants who seemed to run it. Or maybe there just seemed a lot; she just wasn't used to having someone rushing to provide her every whim.

Mr and Mrs Walker were out at a charity luncheon when she arrived, so Brian was the one to show her to her bedroom.

'It's the best guest-room we have,' he told her with pride.

It certainly was lovely, and it had its own bathroom, a luxury Robyn had never known in her life before, usually having to fight Billy in the morning for the use of their one bathroom.

'You'll be meeting my brothers later,' Brian told her. 'They're both invited over for dinner. They're both married, so they'll be bringing their wives.'

It sounded like a nice cosy family dinner, something she had been hoping to avoid. 'I hope your mother hasn't gone to any trouble on my account,' she said awkwardly.

'Not at all,' Brian assured her hastily. 'We're having a party here tonight anyway.'

'A party?' Her heart sank in dismay.

He nodded. 'It's my parents' thirty-fifth wedding anniversary today.'

'Oh, Brian!' she groaned. 'Why didn't you tell me? I haven't even bought them anything.'

'They aren't expecting anything.' He looked a little bashful. 'When you said you'd like to come down this weekend I didn't dare mention my parents' anniversary, just in case you decided not to come.'

'I would have done.'

He grinned. 'That's what I thought. It's only a little party, Robyn, only about fifty or so people.'

'Fifty . . .!' she echoed in a squeaky voice. 'That's a *little* party?'

'By our standards, yes. Usually it would have been a couple of hundred, but my mother hasn't been too well lately. They've got used to my going to drama school, by the way,' he added excitedly.

'They have?' That surprised her; it was only a few weeks since they had been completely against it.

'Well . . .' he hesitated, 'more or less. 'If it doesn't work out after a year I'm expected to follow tradition.'

Robyn raised her eyebrows. 'What do they mean by "work out"?'

He grimaced. 'If I can stick it, I suppose. It's quite hard work, you know.'

'I can imagine. Could you take me shopping this

afternoon so that I can buy your parents a present?'
The big box of chocolates in her case would hardly do
as an anniversary present. They had been intended as a
thank-you for the weekend. What on earth could she
buy this wealthy couple for their anniversary?

'It isn't necessary——'

'It is,' she said firmly. 'Now come on.'

In the end she bought a tiny piece of Staffordshire
china—Brian assured her that his mother collected it,
and Mrs Walker did seem genuinely pleased with the
gift when Robyn gave it to her shortly before dinner.

The senior Walkers had come as something of a surprise to her; she had expected Mrs Walker to be an
overwhelmingly bossy person, her husband equally
forceful. Instead of which she found Alice Walker to be
a fragile woman, still beautiful despite her fifty-five
years, her quiet firmness managing her arrogant husband much more harmoniously than insistence would
have done. John Walker wasn't as she had expected
either, although he was a supremely confident individual. But he was still very much in love with his wife,
and not afraid to show it, was proud of the fact that she
had given him three strapping sons to carry on the
Walker name.

Brian's brothers were something else, both a little too
full of their own importance for Robyn's liking, both a
little on the snobbish side. Andrew was married to
Dulcie, a woman confident in her own beauty and the
power it gave her over her husband, and Richard's wife
was the opposite. June wasn't at all confident in herself.
Of the two Robyn preferred June.

Dinner wasn't at all what she had expected; she was
accepted at the table as if it were nothing unusual for
Brian to have a girl-friend to dinner. And maybe it
wasn't.

Shortly after the meal Mr Walker and his two oldest

sons began a discussion on some medical matter. Brian moved to Robyn's side, grimacing slightly. 'It's always like this,' he groaned.

'Not always, Brian,' Dulcie put in in a disapproving voice. 'And you could do a lot worse than follow Andrew and Richard's example.'

'Could I?' He didn't appear impressed by his sister-in-law's superior attitude. 'I don't see how.'

Dulcie was a natural blonde, and her fair skin flushed with anger, her blue eyes hard. 'I would say acting is a lot worse,' she snapped. 'Wouldn't you, June?'

Small, dark-haired, with nervous brown eyes, June seemed lost among this forceful family, her only ally appearing to be the mild Mrs Walker. 'I—I don't know. Surely it depends what Brian wants——'

'Of course it doesn't,' Dulcie interrupted disgustedly. 'At the moment he *thinks* he wants to be an actor, next year it will be something else. He'll probably join one of those ghastly pop-groups.'

'Don't be silly,' he grinned. 'I'm too old. If you're over nineteen you're over the hill in the pop world.'

Robyn joined in his humour, receiving a look of irritation from Dulcie.

'I think your mother and father should make you enter the medical profession,' Dulcie continued. 'At least it would steady you.'

'It doesn't seem to have done much for Oliver,' Brian replied angrily.

'What happened to Oliver wasn't his fault. Some women just can't take the pressure of being involved with a doctor, especially ones as famous as Oliver.'

'Then how do you explain Melinda leaving him for another doctor?' Brian scorned.

'Because she didn't have any sense,' June cut in. 'And I would rather you didn't discuss my brother in this way.'

Robyn looked at the other girl in surprise, although no one else seemed surprised by this sudden roar from the mouse. She looked at the older girl with new respect, realising that she had misjudged June. June was more like Alice Walker than any of her natural children were, she only roared when it was really necessary.

'Sorry,' Brian muttered.

'So you should be,' Dulcie snapped. 'Poor Oliver, I feel so sorry for him.'

'I doubt he needs it,' June said dryly.

Dulcie gave her a look of feigned innocence. 'Will he be bringing Sheila tonight?'

'Of course—she is my sister-in-law.'

Robyn had no idea who Oliver, Melinda, or Sheila were, but this Oliver came over as rather a fickle young man. Someone called Melinda had walked out on him and he had quickly replaced her with someone called Sheila. He didn't sound exactly the constant type himself, and he didn't sound anything like June either.

'Interesting bunch, aren't they?' Brian said teasingly once June and Dulcie had moved away.

Robyn grinned. 'I like them.'

'So do I, although they can be a little overwhelming en masse. June surprised you, hmm?' he added with some amusement.

She nodded, not realising Brian had been watching her that closely. 'A little,' she admitted.

Brian chuckled. 'She frightens Richard to death.'

'I don't believe that,' she laughed.

'Oh, but she does. June may be quiet, unobtrusive in some ways, but if you cross her . . . Dulcie and I got off quite lightly tonight. June worships her brother and can't bear any criticism of him. When she gets angry, boy, do you know it!'

'Was this Oliver married to Melinda?' Her curiosity had been aroused now.

'Not quite,' Brian said meaningly.

'Oh!' she blushed.

'You see—Oh damn,' he muttered. 'My father wants us to go and greet the guests with them. Come on.' He took hold of her arm.

'Not me, Brian,' she refused. 'I—I'd rather stay here in the background.' She didn't want to appear like part of the family.

'But—Oh damn,' he swore again. 'Look, I have to go. I wish you'd come with me.'

Robyn shook her head, her expression firm before he turned away in defeat. Robyn watched him take his place with the rest of the family, saw Dulcie make some comment to him and then Brian's snapping reply.

Robyn turned away with a smile, well able to imagine that Dulcie had made some comment about her absence. She had been right to be wary of this visit; the Walker family were turning out to be just as socially out of her reach as she had thought they would be. She had known they were quite rich by Brian's way of dress and the expensive sports car he drove, but seeing the whole family together like this, the way they entertained, she was convinced that Brian wasn't the right boy for her.

Still, at least she was dressed up to their standard; her dress was a new purchase for this weekend, a royal blue velvet that reached just below her knees. The shade of blue made her hair look like spun gold, her eyes a deep purple.

She received one or two speculative looks, but no one was curious enough to actually question her presence here. She just smiled brightly when anyone looked her way, slightly relieved when Brian could at last rejoin her.

'Everyone here now?' she asked with a smile, sure that there were more than fifty people here already.

'Everyone,' he nodded. 'Oh, except Sheila and Oliver.'

He shrugged. 'Perhaps they won't come, they aren't really very sociable at the moment.'

As they sounded like newlyweds that wasn't surprising. They probably only needed each other right now.

Robyn was talking to June, a June now as quiet and subdued as she had been when they were first introduced, making the other, fiercer June seem like a figment of the imagination, when the most beautiful woman Robyn had ever seen entered the room.

On closer inspection her looks were striking rather than beautiful; her hair like a deep red flame as it fell in soft waves to her shoulders, her make-up was dark, accentuating her classical features, the black dress she wore fell silkily smooth over her slender curves, her legs were long and silky.

She seemed very confident of herself, although her eyes moved nervously about the room, resting briefly on Robyn before passing on to June, her face breaking into a relieved smile.

'My sister-in-law,' June murmured. 'Come and meet her, Robyn,' she invited.

This was Sheila? Then where was Oliver? That question was soon answered.

'He's been delayed,' Sheila told them in her huskily attractive voice. 'But he shouldn't be long.'

June nodded. 'This is Robyn, Brian's friend.'

Green eyes focused on Robyn before Sheila held out her hand. 'I'm glad to meet you.'

'Would it be too much to ask what delayed Oliver?' June asked in a waspish voice.

Sheila shrugged. 'You know Oliver.'

His sister's mouth tightened. 'Better than anyone. It really is too bad of him, Alice and John are two of his oldest friends. He hasn't left town again, has he?'

'Not that I know of,' Sheila replied smoothly. 'Calm down, June, I'm sure he'll be here.'

Robyn moved tactfully away. The absent Oliver certainly seemed to cause the women in his life a lot of concern. He sounded a very selfish individual.

She wasn't really enjoying this party. Half the guests seemed to be doctors, and the other half seemed to be their wives! She was surprised Brian didn't just give in to pressure and accept the medical profession as his career. She had an idea the supposed acting career was what Dulcie had said it was, a whim on Brian's part to be independent, to do something totally different from the other members of his family.

She froze to the spot as she turned and saw the man walking purposefully across the room towards the senior Walkers, a man totally different from the man full of shadows that she had come to know at Orchard House. This man walked with long relaxed strides, wore a suit of the finest cut and material, his shirt was made of silk, his hair impeccably groomed.

And yet it was Rick, a Rick she hardly recognised. He looked nothing like the man she had come to know and love, the man in the ragged clothing and untidy hair. Now he looked self-assured and sophisticated, wore his fine clothing with an air of breeding that she had never noticed before. And his ribs obviously no longer bothered him; his movements were easy and relaxed.

Robyn stepped back out of sight, watching him greet his host and hostess, talking to them for several minutes before moving to join June and Sheila.

'Hi.'

Robyn turned with a start, smiling her relief when she saw it was Brian standing next to her. 'Hello,' she greeted jerkily.

His arm went about her shoulders. 'I've been looking for you everywhere.'

And she had been looking at Rick, was still looking

at him, unable to believe he was actually here. He looked
so different, not at all like the man she had fallen in
love with. And what was he doing at so distinguished a
gathering—and looking completely at home here too!

'The man talking to June . . .' she began, biting her
bottom lip to stop it trembling. 'Who is he?'

Brian looked over in his sister-in-law's direction. 'With
June? Ah, yes,' he nodded, 'that's Oliver.'

She swallowed hard. 'Oliver . . .?'

'Oliver Pendleton, June's brother. The most distinguished guest we have here.'

Robyn felt as if the world were closing in around her,
as if all reality were fading and just this terrible night-
mare were taking over. The chances of her seeing Rick
this weekend must have been about a million to one,
and yet here he was, and he wasn't Rick Howarth at all.
'Distinguished . . .?' she echoed dully, looking at Rick/
Oliver with new eyes, seeing the self-assurance and
arrogance that came as naturally to him as breathing.

Brian took a couple of drinks off the tray the waiter
was taking round, handing one to Robyn. 'He's a
specialist, a famous one, writes books about it and
everything. Even my father consults him about some of his
patients,' he added as if that were a great honour for any
man. 'Now that Oliver's finally here we're going to drink a
toast to my parents,' he indicated the champagne in their
glasses.

Rick was the one to propose the toast, his voice just
as Robyn remembered it, the lazy amusement edged
with the sword thrust. His words of congratulations
were witty and amusing, judging by the reaction of the
other guests, but Robyn didn't hear one of them.

The fact that the Rick she had thought she was in
love with was actually Oliver Pendleton was bad enough,
but that he was also married to the beautiful Sheila was
something she would never be able to forgive.

CHAPTER SEVEN

ALL the time he had been making love to her he had been married to Sheila, had a wife—a beautiful wife with whom she couldn't hope to compete. No wonder he had been loath to get involved with her, had tried to show her he wasn't interested in a relationship with her. What man would be with a wife like that!

And no wonder the name Oliver Pendleton had seemed so familiar to her. He was indeed a writer, he had been the author of that huge medical volume that had fallen on her toe that day at the library.

Then why had he lived in the village as Rick Howarth? Why had he looked and dressed the way he did? Whatever the answers to those questions, he had lied to her, deceived her when he told her he didn't have a wife, and the man she loved no longer existed. He had been replaced by the haughty Oliver.

'Would you like to meet him?'

She blinked dazedly up at Brian, the significance of his words slowly sinking into her numbed brain. 'No!' she said sharply. 'I—He—He looks busy.' Talking to his wife!

'He's only talking to Sheila,' Brian dismissed. 'Come on. Most of my girl-friends can't wait to get an introduction to him.'

So she had been right, her being here as Brian's girl-friend was nothing unusual to his family. But Brian had just reminded her of something, she was here as *his* girl-friend. With that as a shield she had no need to fear this meeting with Rick. Besides, she doubted she could go on avoiding him all evening.

She allowed Brian to guide her over to where Rick

was now talking to June, Sheila having moved away to talk to some other people.

'If you weren't my brother,' June was saying vehemently, 'I'd tell you just how despicable your manners really are!'

Rick's mouth twisted wryly. 'You aren't doing too badly now,' he drawled.

'I can do better.'

'I'm sure you can,' he taunted.

'If it were my party I wouldn't even let you in at this late hour,' June stormed at him.

He shrugged. 'If it were your party I probably wouldn't even be here.'

June looked ready to explode. 'Well, I like that! You——'

'Calm down, little sister,' Rick sighed. 'You know damn well I never attend these functions. I only made tonight the exception because Alice and John are celebrating a special occasion.'

'You——'

'Time we interrupted, I think,' Brian whispered to Robyn. 'June will never win against Oliver—no one does.'

Remembering the way he had always defeated her she could sympathise with June. Brian was right, June didn't stand a chance of winning.

'May we interrupt?' said Brian with a smile.

Rick turned to look at him, not having seen Robyn yet, she was sure. 'You can not only interrupt,' he drawled, 'you can take my sister away.'

'Don't worry,' she snapped. 'I'm going!' She walked off in the direction of her husband.

Rick watched her go. 'Richard isn't going to know what hit him,' he said with amusement.

Brian grinned. 'He very rarely does. I'd like you to meet my girl-friend, Oliver. This is——'

'Robyn,' she interrupted softly. 'Robyn Castle.'

Rick turned shocked grey eyes on her, his expression quickly masked as he controlled the emotion. 'Miss Castle,' he said tautly, giving nothing away from his manner.

'Mr Pendleton,' she nodded, challenge in her sparkling blue eyes.

'Just Oliver,' he said abruptly.

She made no reply, looking at him calmly. But if she hoped to unnerve him she was disappointed; he just looked steadily back at her.

'Brian,' he turned to the younger man, 'would you mind getting Robyn and me a drink—we both seem to have finished our champagne.'

'Sure.' Brian left them willingly.

Robyn drew a ragged breath. Being left alone with him was the last thing she had expected. 'He didn't ask what you wanted.'

'He knows my tastes,' Rick said curtly.

'How nice!'

'Robyn, what the hell are you doing here?' he rasped, pulling her to one side, out of the focus of curious eyes.

She looked at him with feigned innocence, shaking off his hold on her arm. 'I thought Brian had just explained that, Mr Pendleton. I'm here as his partner.'

'Robyn——'

'Miss Castle,' she said pointedly.

'Like hell I'll call you Miss Castle,' he exploded. 'God, I couldn't believe it when I turned round and saw you standing there!'

Neither had she, but at least she had had time to collect her thoughts together; Rick had had no time at all. But he was controlled—God, was he controlled! And she hated him for it.

'I'm sorry if I surprised you——'

'Surprised me?' He raised his eyes heavenwards at the

understatement. 'I've thought of nothing but you for weeks, and now here you are.'

'Yes,' she gave a brittle smile, 'here I am. Brian is very nice, isn't he?'

Rick's mouth tightened. 'How did you meet him?'

She shrugged. 'At a disco. You do know what a disco is, don't you?' she asked insultingly.

'Yes, I know,' he rasped harshly, her meaning not lost on him. 'Believe it or not, I've even been to a couple.'

'Really?'

'Yes, really! God, Robyn . . .' he groaned, his eyes kindling to warmth, 'I've missed you.'

She hardened her heart to the seduction in his voice, reprimanding herself for still finding him attractive. This man had made a fool of her in the cruellest way possible, had deceived her whole family. He had even had her mother cooking for him because she felt sorry for him! Well, she wasn't falling into that trap again—let him go back to his wife, or some other woman who didn't mind sharing him.

'I take it your ribs have healed.' She ignored the passion in his eyes, determined to fight her attraction to him.

'Finally,' he nodded. 'Robyn, that night——'

'Yes, that night,' she cut in with a derisive laugh. 'People are apt to do and say things out of character at that time of the morning.'

Rick's eyes narrowed. 'You're saying you made a mistake telling me you love me?'

Her laugh was more forced this time. 'Did I really say that? Goodness,' she gave a coy smile, 'how forward of me! Tell me, Mr Pendleton, what field do you specialise in?' She made an effort to look interested in the answer.

'Obstetrics,' he replied curtly.

'Oh.' She blushed; this was the last field she would

have thought, and she instantly felt jealous of all those women he must see every day.

'I enjoy bringing new life into the world,' he said dryly.

Robyn bit her lip, as a new thought occurred to her. 'Do you have any children of your own?'

'No.'

'You sound very sure,' she said bitchily.

'I am. Robyn——'

'Here we are,' Brian arrived back with their drinks. 'I had some trouble finding you,' he added almost accusingly.

Rick took his drink from the other man. 'I wanted to get out of the crush,' he said smoothly. 'Robyn very kindly agreed to keep me company.'

'Poor Robyn's been thrown in at the deep end with my family.' Brian put his arm affectionately about her shoulder. 'It wasn't the way I wanted her to meet you all.'

Rick's rapier-sharp gaze passed slowly over them both. 'Am I to understand that congratulations are in order?' he asked curtly, his eyes cold.

'I——'

'Don't jump the gun, Oliver,' Brian warned, smiling. 'I'm still trying to persuade Robyn that I'm the right man for her. She says it's too soon to tell.'

Rick took a large swallow of his whisky, seeming to feel nothing as the raw alcohol passed down his throat. 'Is it too soon, Robyn?' he suddenly asked her.

She bit her lip, wishing she could look away from him, but found herself mesmerised, as usual. How dared he taunt her with her impetuous declaration of love for him! Her eyes sparkled angrily. 'I think you have to know a person for some time before knowing whether or not you love them,' she told him coldly. 'Anything else can only be called infatuation.'

His jaw tightened. 'You really believe that?'

No, she didn't believe that; she knew deep in her heart that love can strike in an instant, that it can exist where it has no right to be. 'I think I do, Mr Pendleton,' she returned tautly. 'A lot of women have been temporarily attracted by good looks and surface charm, but it takes time—a lot of time,' she added emphatically, 'to really know and love someone.'

'I'm sure *you* would never be infatuated.'

She looked at him unflinchingly, meeting the mockery in his eyes head-on. 'It has been known.'

'But not this time,' Brian put in cheerfully, sensing none of the undercurrents to this conversation. 'Robyn already knows how I feel about her, I'm hoping she'll soon admit to feeling the same way about me. In fact,' he added conspiratorially, 'I'm hoping to persuade her into letting me tell my parents before the end of this weekend.'

Rick raised his eyebrows as he looked at Robyn. 'You're staying here with Alice and John?'

'Just until tomorrow,' she nodded.

'When you'll return home?'

'Yes,' she acknowledged tightly.

'Oliver was in your part of the country a few weeks ago.' Brian spoke again, still completely ignorant of the fact that Robyn and Rick had met before—and Robyn hoped he stayed that way! 'In fact it was because of that that my parents thought of my aunt and uncle when they decided I should go away for a while.'

'I saw Jim and Wilma several times while I was there,' Rick nodded. 'I doubt your parents thought you would come back from there and announce your intention of getting married,' he said dryly.

'He hasn't done that, Mr Pendleton,' Robyn told him abruptly. 'At least, not with me in mind.'

'I—Oh damn,' Brian scowled. 'My mother's calling me again.'

Rick smiled unsympathetically. 'That's what happens when your parents are the ones giving the party.'

Brian grimaced. 'I have to go and say goodnight to one of my aunts.' He kissed Robyn briefly on the lips. 'I'll be back as soon as I can,' he promised.

'Let's get out of here.' Rick instantly pulled Robyn towards the door, out of the room and down the corridor, to push her inside another room, closing and locking the door behind them. 'Now,' he said softly, 'I want to hear more about this *infatuation*.'

He had warned her he could be dangerous, and now he was dangerous in another kind of way; his anger was making him so.

'Well?' he rasped.

Robyn backed away from him. 'Will you please open the door?' She faced him defiantly. 'People will wonder what we're doing in here.'

'No one will wonder anything, because no one saw us come in here. And even if they had, I couldn't give a damn what they think.'

'You may not, but I—Rick, let me go!' she cried as he reached out and twisted her arm behind her back, pulling her close against him.

'Ah,' he said softly, his breath stirring the hair at her temple. 'So it's Rick again now, and not Mr Pendleton.'

She held herself rigid, refusing to give in to the stirrings of his body. 'Pendleton is your name,' she pointed out stiffly.

'So is Richard Howarth.'

'It is?' She blinked up at him, instantly wishing she hadn't as her gaze was met and held by hard grey eyes.

'Oliver Richard Howarth Pendleton,' he reeled off his full name.

'How grand!' she taunted. 'And why were you Rick Howarth in Sanford?'

He shrugged. 'I hardly looked like Oliver Pendleton, now did I?'

'Hardly,' she agreed dryly.

'So I became Rick Howarth.'

'What a nice little trick' she taunted bitterly.

He gave an impatient sigh, 'It wasn't a trick, Robyn——'

'Funny—it fooled me.' She turned away, wishing he would let her go. She wasn't sure how much longer she could hold out against him if he continued to hold her like this.

'Oh, Robyn, Robyn!' His arms tightened about her. 'I didn't do it to fool anyone. I needed time alone, to think, and as Rick Howarth I could do that. You see, I was engaged to be married, and——'

'Oh yes,' she cut in, 'I heard about that.' And she had also heard of his marriage soon afterwards.

He frowned. 'You did?'

She shrugged. 'Someone mentioned it.'

His mouth twisted. 'I'm sure they did. Dulcie, right?'

'I think so, I'm not sure.' At the time she hadn't been particularly interested, not realising they were talking about Rick.

'It was Dulcie,' he said with certainty. 'She takes an unhealthy interest in other people's lives. She should have a baby, that would keep her occupied.'

'A man's answer to everything!'

His eyes darkened in colour, his breathing was shallow. 'Not everything, Robyn,' he said huskily. 'God, I've missed you. You'll never know what it cost me to leave you in Sanford.'

Robyn drew a ragged breath. 'The price of a taxi to the station, I should think,' she said sharply.

'No! Robyn——'

'Will you let me go!' She couldn't stand being next to him like this any more. 'Or do I have to scream?' She

looked up at him challengingly, wishing it didn't bring
her quite so close to the firmness of his mouth. If he
should bend his head even slightly . . .

He must have seen the apprehension in her eyes and
realised the reason for it, because at that moment he did
exactly what she most dreaded, and moved his lips
slowly against hers, savouring each touch, releasing her
arm to hold her gently to the hard length of his body,
moaning softly in his throat as her arms went involun-
tarily about him.

His mouth at once hardened on hers, caressing her
lips apart to deepen and lengthen the kiss. When he
raised his head Robyn leant weakly against him. 'I didn't
hear you scream,' his voice was husky.

'No.'

'Robyn, I was wrong in Sanford,' he told her earn-
estly. 'Wrong to leave you as I did. It doesn't really
matter that I'm so much older than you. After eight
weeks of being apart from you I still want you as badly
as I did then. I won't fight you any more, Robyn. I just
want you back in my life.' He placed impassioned kisses
down her slender throat.

It would be so easy to give in, to accept a Rick who
suddenly seemed to want her as badly as she wanted
him. But she couldn't forget Sheila, and she wasn't the
type the 'other woman' was made of.

She pulled away from him, her heart breaking anew.
She finally had what she had always wanted, Rick eager
and willing, and she had to be the one to say no, to
reject him this time.

'Please—Mr Pendleton.' She saw his head flinch back
at the formal way she addressed him. 'I don't know
what the usual reaction is to such a proposition,' she
said coldly, 'but mine is no.'

'You don't understand. I want——'

'I understand exactly what you want!' she cut in

shrilly. 'And it wouldn't matter what you offered, the answer would still be no.'

He drew a deep controlling breath, his gaze searching her set features. 'You don't love me?'

Robyn shook her head. 'I don't think I ever did. In case you didn't notice, Sanford is a very small place, not exactly exciting. You were new, a mystery, and I——'

'You wanted to probe that mystery,' he finished tautly. 'What was the routine, get me into bed with you and hope that I would tell all?'

She refused to flinch at the scorn in his voice, holding her head proudly erect. 'And now I know all without having to go to bed with you.'

His mouth twisted. 'Are you telling me you wouldn't have enjoyed that part of it?'

Colour quickly invaded her cheeks even though she tried to stop it. 'I'm not denying I found you attractive——'

'You would be a liar if you did!'

'Yes, I'd be a liar! But then you know a lot about lying, don't you,' she accused bitterly. 'Just what were you doing in Sanford?'

'Writing.'

She frowned. 'Your medical books——'

'No,' he shook his head, 'not a medical book. At least, not a non-fiction one. I've been trying my hand at fiction with a medical background.'

'Did you have to look like a tramp for that?' she snapped.

Anger fired in his eyes. 'As a matter of fact, yes. My main character was a man who found he had six months to live if he didn't have a certain operation. He decided he wouldn't have it—until he fell in love with a girl he met when he went off to be alone.'

Robyn paled. 'You used me!' she gasped.

'No——'

'Yes! My God, you're a bastard! How dare you use me as copy for a book?'

'I didn't "use" you in any way,' he scorned. 'I didn't ask you to intrude into my life the way you did. I was trying to work—having a curious teenager about all the time wasn't something I welcomed.'

'I noticed.'

'Then you must see I didn't use you for my book. The girl Dominic met was nothing like you. She was a damn sight older, for one thing.'

'But you still made love to me. You—Don't you have any morals?'

'Of course I have morals——'

'You don't know the meaning of the word!' she snapped.

'In my book morality means loyalty to one person.'

'Yes!' she glared at him.

'Then why the hell can't you be loyal to me?' he rasped.

'Because—because—Oh, let me out of here!' She brushed past him, turning the key in the lock and wrenching the door open. 'One woman may not be enough for you,' she turned to shout at him, 'but one man is enough for me—and that's Brian.'

'Robyn——'

'*Leave—me—alone!*' She wrenched away from him, running back to the room containing the other guests.

She was shaking with reaction, avidly searching for Brian as she sensed Rick behind her. Brian didn't take much finding, he was looking for her too.

'Where on earth have you been?' he frowned.

'I—I went upstairs to get a handkerchief,' she invented, her movements jerky as she dared to glance behind her. Rick was standing near the door, his eyes narrowed as he watched them, his expression enigmatic.

'You should have told me,' Brian brought her attention back to him. 'I could have come with you,' he added meaningfully.

She raised her eyebrows. 'I don't think your parents would have approved of that.'

'Maybe not,' he grinned. 'But I would.'

Sheila had joined Rick now and was talking to him quietly. They seemed to be leaving. Robyn heaved a sigh of relief. She hoped Sheila didn't know anything of her husband's behaviour either eight weeks ago or now.

'Robyn!'

She dragged her gaze back from Rick with effort, aware that this would be the last time she ever saw him. 'Yes, Brian?' she asked absently.

'I—Oh, never mind!' He gave an impatient sigh. 'What do you keep looking at?'

'Nothing.' She bit her lip. 'I—I think your mother wants you again.' She had noticed Mrs Walker's frantic glances in their direction.

'For God's sake!' He looked angrily at his mother. 'Someone else to say goodnight to! You can come with me this time,' he took hold of her hand, 'I'm not going to risk losing you again.'

Robyn looked over in dismay to where Rick and his wife were talking to Brian's parents. 'I'd rather wait here,' she told him. 'I promise I won't move.'

'You're coming with me!'

He wouldn't be denied, and pulled her along with him. Robyn looked down at her hands as Brian made a joking farewell to Rick.

'Goodnight, Miss Castle.'

Her head jerked back at the sound of that softly mocking voice. 'Mr Pendleton,' she said in a stilted voice, her gaze stopping at the top button of his shirt.

'I enjoyed meeting you, Robyn,' Sheila Pendleton

spoke now. 'Brian assures me I shall be seeing a lot of you.'

She looked at Brian, seeing the pride and love shining in his bright blue eyes. Pride and love that she had no right to nurture. After this weekend she couldn't see Brian again, not still loving Rick as she did.

'Perhaps, Mrs Pendleton,' she answered noncommittally.

'I hope so,' the other woman smiled. 'Don't you, Oliver?' She looked up lovingly at her husband.

Rick's expression was shuttered. 'I have no doubt we shall all be seeing Robyn again.'

Brian's arm tightened about her shoulders. 'I wish I had your confidence, Oliver,' he said ruefully.

'I don't think you need confidence, Brian,' Rick drawled. 'Robyn assures me she's a one-man woman.'

Brian looked down at her eagerly. 'Did you? Did you really?'

She licked her lips, shooting Rick a resentful glance from beneath lowered lashes. 'Not exactly, Brian,' she let him down lightly. 'I believe I told Mr Pendleton that I believe in being loyal to the person you're with.' She would have liked to have added something cutting to Rick, but she was too conscious of his wife standing at his side, a woman too nice to have to put up with the rake Rick undoubtedly was.

'And you're the man of the moment,' Rick drawled insultingly to Brian. 'I should make the most of it—women are inclined to be fickle, especially ones as young as Robyn.'

'Not fickle,' Robyn flashed. 'Just choosy.'

If she had hoped to anger him then he gave no outward sign of it, although the glitter in his eyes promised retribution at some later date. But as they were never to meet again that wouldn't be possible.

She felt somewhat less tense once Rick and his wife

had left, although she wished Brian wouldn't be quite so possessive with her.

'Please, Brian,' she fought against the intimacy of his kisses as they parted later that night. 'Don't,' she added pleadingly.

He had her trapped against the wall outside her bedroom. 'No one will know if I come into your room with you,' he murmured softly. 'I'll leave before the maid brings your tea in the morning.'

She had a feeling this plan had been carried out many times before. 'Brian——'

'No one will know,' he repeated huskily, his lips on her throat.

'I will.' She squirmed against him, wishing her movements didn't excite him even further, the hardness of his thighs pressed against her.

'Don't be such a prude, Robyn!' He was becoming angry now, increasingly so as she thwarted his plans for the night ahead. 'No one waits until they're married any more.'

'Maybe if I were going to marry you I wouldn't wait either.' She pushed him away from her, frightened of the glazed passion in his eyes, the excited flush to his cheeks.

Seen like this, the likeable companion of the past weeks seemed not to exist; an immature sexual satisfaction was Brian's only aim at the moment.

'I said no, Brian!' she said vehemently.

'Why?' His mouth was sulkily angry. 'I bet if it had been Oliver you wouldn't have said no.'

Robyn went white at his accusation. 'What did you say?' she exploded.

He put his hands moodily into his pockets, his expression rebellious. 'You heard me,' he muttered.

'But what did you mean by it?' Surely she hadn't given herself away, revealed her secret love for Rick?

'I saw the way the two of you kept looking at each

other,' Brian snarled. 'You aren't Oliver's usual type, I must admit, but he liked you, I could tell.'

Robyn licked her lips, her hands kneading together. 'Does he have a type?' she asked softly, dreading the answer.

'Oh yes,' Brian sneered. 'Usually they look like Melinda and Sheila.'

She frowned. 'Like Sheila? But——'

'Women like that don't make claims,' he scorned. 'And Oliver likes his freedom. Melinda was the only one who came anywhere near holding him, and now she's gone,' he shrugged dismissively.

'Gone?' Her mouth felt dry, her hands shook.

'Dead,' Brian revealed callously.

Robyn seemed to sway where she stood. 'Dead?' she echoed faintly.

He nodded. 'About six months ago.'

And since then he had married Sheila. Could he possibly love Sheila or had he married her out of a sense of loss? Melinda had meant something to him, too much, surely, for him to have fallen in love again so soon.

'You are interested in Oliver, aren't you?' Brian persisted angrily.

'No.' She was aware that her denial lacked conviction, but her thoughts were still with Rick and the woman he had loved. But what of the woman he was now married to? Sheila Pendleton seemed well aware of her husband's faults, and she accepted them. Robyn knew she would never be brave enough to accept his other women, especially as she *was* the other woman.

'Liar!' Brian snapped. 'God—I bring my girl-friend home and she falls for a family friend, a man old enough to be her father!'

'He is not!' she instantly defended. 'Thirty-six isn't old.'

Brian's eyes narrowed suspiciously. 'How do you know Oliver is thirty-six?'

'I——'

'My God,' Brian said slowly, 'the two of you have met before. You have, haven't you?' he accused resentfully.

Colour flooded her cheeks. 'No! No, of course we haven't. Look, I think I should go to my room now, we don't want to disturb the rest of the household.'

'They'll all be asleep by now,' but he lowered his voice nonetheless.

'But I agree with you about going to your room, we haven't finished this conversation yet.' He opened the door and pushed her inside. 'We can talk more comfortably in here. Now, how well did—*do* you know Oliver?'

'I don't know him at all.' She moved to switch on the bedside lamp, more for something to do than add extra light to the overhead light, Brian having switched it on when they entered the room. And she wasn't lying when she said she didn't know Rick, she really didn't.

'Then why won't you marry me?'

'Because I don't love you,' she sighed. 'And that has nothing to do with Ri—Oliver—I mean, Mr Pendleton.' Her protests were falling on deaf ears, she could tell that. And it was all her own fault, she was making a mess of things. 'It has nothing to do with anything but the fact that I don't love you,' she added to try and convince him.

Brian eyed her suspiciously. 'There's something you aren't telling me.'

'No, nothing——'

'Yes. Oliver was in your area a few weeks ago, before he was ill——'

'Ill?' she echoed sharply. 'You mean his ribs?'

'You do know each other! There's no other way you

could know about Oliver's broken ribs.'

'I—He—he could have mentioned it this evening,' she said desperately.

'No way,' Brian shook his head. 'It isn't the sort of topic he would bring up at a party, it isn't the sort of thing he would talk about at all.'

Robyn bit her lip, knowing he was right. 'Then someone else must have mentioned it.'

'Who?'

'I—Dulcie—Yes, I think it was Dulcie.'

'Never,' Brian derided. 'She may be a doctor's wife, but any form of ill-health sickens her. Dulcie wouldn't have told you anything about Oliver's stay in hospital.'

'But he didn't stay in hospital! I mean——'

'You mean he didn't stay in hospital that you know of,' Brian finished with a sigh. 'It's all right, Robyn, you don't have to pretend any longer, I know when to accept defeat.'

She looked at him pleadingly. 'It isn't like you think. I admit I did meet Oliver before. But I—Nothing happened.' Not quite!

Brian looked as if she had hit him. 'I loved you, Robyn,' he choked.

She didn't think now was the time to point out that he was already using the past tense, touching his arm understandingly. 'I'm sorry, Brian.'

'Was he the man?'

'The man?' She looked startled.

He nodded. 'The one you told me about when we first met.'

Robyn swallowed hard. 'Would it do any good to deny it?'

'No.'

'Then I won't,' she sighed.

'What happened?'

She shrugged. 'Nothing. He just left. I—I understand

why now. There's who he is, and——and Sheila.'

'Mm, she's a responsibility Oliver wouldn't shirk. He came back because she needed him, she gets very depressed.'

That didn't surprise Robyn. She would get very depressed too if she couldn't trust the man she was married to.

'But who Oliver is doesn't count,' Brian continued. 'He's just as happy when people don't know who he is. Happier, actually. He lives like a recluse most of the time.'

'I noticed!'

The glimmer of a smile lightened Brian's features; his disappointment was shortlived. It showed that his feelings hadn't been deeply involved, no matter what he claimed to the contrary. Robyn had the feeling she was just another rebellion on his part, a deviation from the sort of girl he was eventually going to pick for a wife.

'He lived that way in Sanford, hmm?'

'He did,' she confirmed. 'But you said he'd been in hospital . . .' she prompted worriedly.

'Well, you already know about his ribs being broken,' his expression was reproachful. 'One of those broken ribs punctured a lung.'

'Oh no!' She felt weak, and sank slowly down on to the bed.

'Hey, I'm sorry!' Brian sat beside her, his arm about her shoulders. 'I didn't mean to upset you.'

'You didn't. I——I just——It was a shock. Was he——very ill?'

'Pretty bad. We thought he was going to die for a while. But he's fine now,' he assured her.

'Was he in hospital long?' God, she thought, Rick had almost died and she hadn't even known about it. He must have done this to himself when he left Sanford so abruptly. Now she knew he had done so to be with his depressed wife. Maybe that was why the letter in the blue envelope had angered him.

'A few weeks. But he's a hundred per cent now. Really,' Brian insisted as she continued to look worried.

'If you say so,' but she still sounded unsure.

'Ask him yourself—No, I don't suppose you can, can you? You didn't exactly seem the best of friends tonight.'

Robyn gave a wan smile. 'We aren't.'

And they weren't ever likely to be again. Rick was completely out of her reach, a married man.

CHAPTER EIGHT

PARTING from Brian the next day wasn't too difficult. He seemed resigned to the fact that she no longer wanted to continue seeing him, unless it was as a friend.

She felt rather embarrassed about facing his parents now that her relationship with Brian had been decided, but Alice and John Walker treated her just as politely as they had the day before, although Robyn felt sure Brian must have told them of their decision.

Brian took her to the station, kissing her on the cheek. 'I'm sorry things didn't work out.'

'So am I.' She gently touched his cheek; she meant what she said, she wished she could have been more than fond of him.

'Here,' he handed her some magazines and chocolates, 'have a nice journey.'

She had a thoughtful one, not necessarily a 'nice' one. She had made an effort to forget Rick with another man, and in doing so had simply met up with him again. Fate must simply be against her. It didn't seem fair; Brian had been such a nice boy too. If only he hadn't known Rick!

But it was no good wishing for what might have been. If she did that she might as well wish that Rick wasn't married, that he had loved her in return. Instead of which she had just been another woman to him. At least he had had the decency not to take her when he had the chance, although she knew it hadn't really been through decency on his part, it had been sheer necessity, the pain of his ribs the only thing that had stopped him. Decency had had nothing to do with it.

'Have a nice time, dear?' her mother wanted to know once she got home. Her father was immersed in the Sunday newspapers, Bill was out as usual.

'Very nice,' she replied noncommittally, and went on to tell her mother about the anniversary party, although she omitted meeting Rick again. Better to just let him continue to fade from all of their lives.

But it was much harder the second time around; her evenings out with Selma had come to an end, through her own choice. They might have been doing her good, but it wasn't fair on any of the boys she might meet, especially if they decided to become serious about her as Brian had.

Selma accepted her decision goodnaturedly. Her sights were now set on Alan Mitchell, a boy who had just started work at the library. Not that he seemed to return her interest, spending more time with Robyn than he did with Selma.

Not that Robyn encouraged him, although she had always liked him when they had been at school together. He had been very good at athletics at school, the boy all the girls wanted to date, although at the time he had been pretty single-minded about a career in athletics, devoting all his time to his training programme, till a serious accident that had broken his pelvis had put an end to that promising future.

Robyn had been surprised when he started work at the library, although he seemed to be enjoying it.

'I've always liked books,' he confided to Robyn one lunchtime. The two of them were sitting in the park, shafts of sunlight filtering through the tree above them. It was the same park Robyn had come to with Rick, but nowadays she forced herself to go to these places. She had even returned to Orchard House a couple of times.

'It must seem strange——' she broke off, biting her tongue for her thoughtlessness. 'I'm sorry,' she mumbled, looking at Alan with distressed eyes.

He gave a rueful smile. 'I know exactly what you were going to say, and I don't mind. You see, it doesn't seem strange to me at all. I never particularly liked athletics——'

'Oh, but you must have done,' she protested. 'You were always so dedicated.'

Alan shook his head. 'No, I wasn't. My father wanted me to be the best athlete in the world, he worked towards that end from the moment I could walk.'

Her eyes were wide. 'Without even asking you?'

He grinned. 'I walked before I talked.'

'You know what I mean!'

'Yes,' he still smiled. 'I loved him, I wanted to make him happy.'

'Yes, but——'

'We're all forced into roles in our lifetime, Robyn.' He sobered. 'Take Selma, for example. She thinks she has to turn every male on that she comes into contact with. She's basically insecure——'

'Selma? Insecure?'

'Yes. She giggles and jokes about, gives you the impression she would go to bed with you at the drop of a hat. But it isn't the truth.'

Robyn blinked, dazed at the sensitivity of this man. At twenty-one he was tall, dark and handsome, had retained his muscular physique despite the fact that he no longer participated in sports. 'It isn't?' she asked huskily.

'No. Selma's a sham. That's the reason she loses her boy-friends so regularly. She's all talk, and underneath that talk she's just an insecure little girl looking for someone to love her.'

'She likes you,' Robyn told him softly.

He sighed. 'Not me, Robyn, the role she remembers me in. The person I really am is vastly different from how she remembers me at school. I'm no hero, just a

man who tried and failed to be the world's best athlete.'
His words were self-derisory.

Robyn's hand moved to cover his. 'You didn't fail! If
it hadn't been for the accident——'

Alan stood up. 'I never think of might-have-beens,
Robyn. They just make you bitter.'

She stood up too. 'Selma doesn't like you for what
you could have been, she likes you for what you are
now.' And Robyn liked him too, liked him for seeing
Selma as she had come to know her, liked him for the
incredible wisdom he seemed to have for one so young.

He shook his head. 'There's no glamour attached to
going out with a cripple.'

'You aren't a cripple!' He limped, one leg was slightly
shorter than the other, but it was hardly noticeable.

'I'm not perfect either.'

'No one is,' Robyn said bitterly.

'A lesson learnt the hard way?'

She blushed. 'Yes. Now, I think we'd better get back.
Mr Leaven doesn't like unpunctuality. And don't say
that's another role, he enjoys laying into me if I'm late.'

Alan laughed. 'But you expect it.'

'Maybe,' she conceded. 'But I wouldn't be too disappointed if just once he forgot.'

Selma greeted her eagerly when she returned. 'Did
you put in a good word for me?' she wanted to know.

She had asked Robyn to try and convince Alan of
how much she liked him, and Robyn had promised to
try. Well, she had tried! 'I couldn't actually come out
and ask him to go out with you, Selma,' she evaded.

'No,' the other girl agreed. 'As long as you mentioned
me.'

'Oh, I did that,' Robyn said with relief.

'Good. I—Oh, I nearly forgot,' Selma gave a rueful
smile. 'You have a visitor.'

'*I* do?'

'Mm,' Selma nodded.

'Billy——'

'It isn't Billy,' Selma grinned. 'He looks suspiciously like your Rick, only tidier, if you know what I mean.'

Yes, she knew what she meant! Panic gripped her, making her shake with reaction. What was Rick doing here? There was only one way to find out the answer to that. 'Where is he?' she asked in a strangulated voice.

'Sitting in one of the armchairs at the back of the library, near the A section. He arrived just after you'd left with Alan, but he said he wanted to wait for you.'

'Thanks, Selma,' she said absently, and turned in the direction of the A section, dreading seeing Rick again and yet finding herself charged with anticipation at the same time.

She had felt only half alive this last week since leaving Brian's parents' house, since last seeing Rick, and just knowing she was to see him once again filled her with pleasure.

The emotion was successfully masked before she confronted Rick, and her expression was cool and remote, although her heart leapt into her throat just at the sight of him. 'Tidier' didn't exactly describe the way he looked—devastating was a more apt description, the charcoal-grey pin-striped suit tailored on to him, his silk shirt snowy white. He bore no resemblance to the old Rick, but looked totally Oliver Pendleton.

Until she looked at his eyes! The expression in those mesmerising grey eyes was totally Rick, slightly narrowed they conveyed better than words the desire he still felt towards her.

He took an involuntary step towards her and then checked himself. 'Robyn . . .' he said huskily.

It took all her will-power not to declare her love for him right then and there, but she managed to control the impulse, if she did but know it looking coolly self-assured in the black fitted skirt and pink blouse.

'Mr Pendleton,' she greeted stiffly.

A smile touched his well-formed mouth. 'So we're still being formal, are we?'

She raised cool questioning eyebrows. 'I have no idea what you mean.'

His mouth quirked. 'You know, Robyn. When you start calling me Rick I'll know that we're friends again.'

'I didn't know we were ever that!'

'Lovers, then,' he shrugged.

Robyn gasped, and looked about them selfconsciously. 'Do you mind!' she hissed.

'Not at all.' He thrust his hands into his trousers pockets, unconsciously pulling the material tautly across his thighs.

'We were never lovers!' she whispered vehemently.

'Weren't we?' He feigned a frown. 'No, we weren't, not quite. Who was the boy you went to lunch with?' he asked suddenly, all teasing gone, his eyes narrowed.

She looked startled. 'Alan?'

Rick nodded tersely. 'I believe that was his name.'

'He——' she hesitated. 'He's my boy-friend,' she invented, hoping Alan would forgive her for forcing him into this role.

Rick's mouth tightened. 'Is he indeed?'

'Yes!' she snapped.

'For a girl who supposedly didn't have even one boy-friend before I met her,' he drawled insultingly, 'you're certainly making up for it.'

Her eyes flashed deeply violet. 'And why shouldn't I? I didn't know anyone had staked a claim on me.'

His fingers curled painfully about her upper arm. '*I* have,' his eyes glittered. 'You're mine, Robyn, and no one—*no one* is going to take you away from me.' His expression was fierce. 'Let alone that kid you just came back with.'

Robyn swallowed hard, thrilled by his masterfulness in spite of herself. Oh, if only he could have been like this before, before she had discovered how despicable he really was! She shook off his arm. 'For your information, Alan is far from being a boy. And I don't belong to you, Mr Pendleton,' she told him coldly. 'Now would you please stay away from me.'

'Never!' he snarled.

'Then I'll have to make you, won't I!'

His mouth curved into a humourless smile, his eyes like chips of ice. 'You can try, Robyn. But I'll wear you down in the end.'

Her mouth set stubbornly. '*You* can try,' she scorned angrily. 'But you won't succeed.'

'I will,' he said with a certainty that frightened Robyn. He touched her briefly on the cheek. 'I'll be seeing you, Robyn.'

'You won't!'

He made no further comment but walked away with a half-smile on his lips, nodding briefly to Selma on his way out.

If she weren't so angry—and this a public library!—she would have screamed with the frustration of this whole meeting. Rick was back in her life, and this time he seemed determined to stay—even if she didn't want him to.

'He gets more handsome every time I see him,' Selma whispered ecstatically at her side.

'He's an arrogant brute!' Robyn hissed.

Selma gave her a knowing look. 'But you love it.'

'I do not!'

'Liar!' Selma smiled before going back to her work.

Robyn stormed through the double doors labelled 'Staff Only', hanging her jacket up in the cloakroom.

Alan came out of the staff-room as she was viciously brushing her hair, two bright spots of angry colour in her cheeks. 'What's happened to you?' he asked in amuse-ment. 'It can't have been Leaven, we weren't late back.'

'Nothing happened to me,' she snapped, still too furious to think straight. Rick thought he just had to snap his fingers and she would come running. Well, she wouldn't, she *couldn't*. The role of mistress was surely the worst one of all.

Alan studied her closely. 'Do you usually get angry at nothing?' he asked gently.

The fight went out of her. 'No,' she sighed, putting away her brush. 'No, I don't. You see I—I just met—well, a sort of ex-boy-friend——'

'Only sort of?'

She blushed. 'Well, he's hardly a boy, you see, and——'

'No, I don't see,' Alan frowned. 'How old is he?'

She shrugged. 'Mid-thirties. But that isn't what bothers me——'

'It bothers me,' Alan said quietly.

Her expression brightened. 'It does?'

'Yes, it—Why?' he asked suspiciously.

Robyn took a deep breath, wondering how he was going to take this next bit of news. 'I told him you were my boy-friend.'

'What!'

She bit her lip guiltily. 'I'm sorry, Alan. You see, he thought we were involved, you and I, so I let him go on believing it.'

'Can I ask why?'

She looked down at her hands. 'He's married, Alan.' She looked up at him pleadingly. 'I didn't know at the time I—I liked him.'

'He didn't tell you,' Alan guessed.

'No.'

'Okay, Robyn, I'll be your boy-friend. Where would you like to go tonight?'

'Nowhere,' she laughed. 'I'll only need you as a verbal boy-friend.' Although it didn't seem to have put Rick off so far!

Alan shrugged. 'Okay. I'd decided to ask Selma out anyway.'

'You had?' Her face lit up as she envisaged Selma's pleasure. And she was sure Alan was wrong about Selma's feelings; she liked him as he was now, not as the school hero he had once been.

'Do you think she'll accept?' he asked uncertainly.

'I—Why don't you ask her and find out?' She decided against telling him how eagerly Selma would accept. After all, the poor girl deserved some secrets.

He nodded. 'I'll do that.'

Robyn felt a little more relaxed now; the last few minutes' conversation with Alan had lessened her anger towards Rick. Not that he was going to walk back into her life and stay. She would tell him any lie to get rid of him, anything at all.

Selma was ecstatic about her date with Alan that evening, and she talked of nothing else all afternoon, so much so that Robyn was glad to leave work that evening.

'What do you think I should wear?' Selma asked as they clattered down the stairs together. Both of them finished at five tonight.

Robyn sighed impatiently. 'We've already discussed this, Selma, several times, in fact. You're going to the cinema, so you wear something casual.'

'Yes, but——'

'I know you look good in your black dress, but it just isn't suitable for wearing at the cinema.'

Selma wrinkled her nose. 'Why couldn't he have asked me to the disco or something?'

'You know he can't dance very easily, it makes his leg ache.'

'Oh dear!' Selma put a hand up to her mouth. 'I just
know I'm going to say something like that tonight and
put my foot in it.'

Robyn shrugged, having listened to similar comments
all afternoon. 'Then maybe you shouldn't have accepted
his invitation.'

'Not accepted?' Selma was scandalised. 'Are you
joking? I've liked Alan ever since we were at school. I
can't believe he's actually asked me out.'

'Believe it,' Robyn advised. 'And wear trousers
tonight.'

'My silk ones?'

'No,' she sighed. 'Use your head, Selma. Alan likes
you in the sort of clothes you wear to work——'

'But——'

'So wear something casual,' Robyn repeated firmly.
'You don't have to impress Alan.' And some of Selma's
more elaborate outfits could just scare him off.

Selma pouted her disappointment. 'Not even my silk
trousers?'

'No,' she laughed.

'Spoilsport!'

'Robyn . . .'

She spun round to confront Rick, the formal suit now
replaced with tight-fitting denims and a loose sweat-
shirt, the neatly combed hair ruffled into disorder. When
he looked like this she could forget he was Oliver
Pendleton, and she only just stopped her joyful smile at
seeing him here.

Selma raised her eyebrows pointedly. 'See you tomorrow, Robyn. Goodnight, Mr Howarth,' she added
with a coy smile in his direction.

He nodded, his smile charming. 'Goodnight, Selma.'

She was obviously delighted that he knew her
name, and moved away with an exaggerated sway of
her hips. But she needn't have bothered for Rick's

benefit, he had eyes only for Robyn.

'What do you want?' she asked rudely.

He appeared unperturbed by her attitude. 'I thought I might give you a lift home.'

'I have my bike here.' She walked round to the side of the library, aware that he followed her, his long and leisurely strides bringing him to her side.

She gasped as she looked down at the back wheel of her bicycle—the tyre was completely flat. He had done this, he had to have done! She turned on him accusingly.

He put up a silencing hand. 'Before you say anything——'

'You did this!' she exploded. 'You let my tyre down.'

Rick calmly shook his head. 'No, I didn't.'

'You——'

'But I sat and watched the two young boys who did,' he revealed lazily, crossing his arms over his chest as she bent down to inspect the wheel.

Robyn turned to glare at him. 'Why didn't you stop them?' She stood up to kick the wheel. 'It's no good, they've taken the valve from my inner tube.'

Rick shook his head. 'They didn't take it, they threw it away. Over there,' he pointed to some thick bushes a short distance away.

She drew an angry breath. 'I suppose you sat and watched them do that too?'

He smiled. 'Yes.'

'But why?' she groaned. 'Now I'll have to get the bus.'

'I've already offered you a lift home.'

Her mouth twisted. 'And I've already refused.'

He shrugged. 'The offer's still there.'

Robyn turned away. 'So is the refusal.' She gave one last angry glare at her bicycle before walking off in the direction of the bus stop. How could he have just watched those boys do that to her bicycle! He had probably put them up to it!

There were half a dozen other people waiting at the bus stop, so she went to the back of the queue, searching through her handbag for the right change.

'Care for a lift, darling?'

She looked up to find a Rolls-Royce outrageously parked at the bus stop, Rick leaning over to talk to her out of the open passenger door. She closed her handbag with a snap, her chin going high. 'No, thank you,' she refused icily, wishing he would stop embarrassing her and just drive on.

'Come on, darling,' he said coaxingly. 'I'm sorry I insulted your mother, but that's no reason to walk off like this.'

Robyn frowned. What on earth was he talking about now? They hadn't so much as mentioned her mother. 'What——'

'Get in the car, darling, and we'll kiss and make up,' Rick added enticingly.

Robyn could see the smiles on the faces of the other people waiting in the queue, and she wasn't about to stand here and be humiliated any longer. She got into the car, slamming the door behind her.

Rick grinned as he accelerated the car away from the pavement in the direction of Robyn's home.

'You swine!' she muttered through gritted teeth, ignoring the fact that this new car of his was much more comfortable than the bus would have been.

He glanced sideways at her. 'For offering you a lift home?'

'For embarrassing me into accepting it.' She refused to look at him. 'That was the idea, wasn't it?'

'Yes,' he told her happily.

'What are you doing here?' she asked in exasperation.

'Visiting you.'

'I don't want any visits from you!'

'Look, I know I walked out on you——'

'You flatter yourself if you think that bothers me!' she snapped.

His hand moved out to cover hers, his fingers tightening as she would have snatched her hand away. 'I would have come back before now, Robyn, but I—I was detained.'

'By Sheila!'

He frowned. 'No, not by Sheila. I admit she was the reason I had to leave in the first place, but she wasn't the reason I stayed away.'

'I don't suppose she was,' Robyn scorned, sure now that Rick couldn't love his wife. But that didn't excuse him wanting an affair with *her*.

'A punctured lung was the reason I couldn't come back straight away,' he told her harshly.

'So I heard.' She hardened her heart, not willing to let him see how the news of his illness had upset her.

'Brian?' he snapped.

'Yes.'

'He has another girl-friend, you know.'

She did know, having spoken to Brian on the telephone yesterday. She nodded. 'Her name's Trudi.'

'Doesn't it bother you?' he rasped.

'Should it?' she returned calmly.

'Obviously not. How far have things gone between you and Alan?' he asked grimly.

Robyn remained cool with effort. 'Mind your own business.'

'*You* are my business.' His eyes were very dark as he turned to look at her, his hand returning to the steering wheel, shaking slightly.

'And Sheila?'

Rick frowned. 'Are you jealous of her?'

'Me, jealous?' she exploded at his audacity. 'I don't have any right to be jealous over anything. Anyway, you aren't worth it.'

'Then why the interest in Sheila?'

'Why not?' she shrugged.

'Robyn . . .!' He gave an impatient sigh. 'Are you still annoyed because I didn't tell you who I really am?'

'The famous obstetrician Oliver Richard Howarth Pendleton?' she taunted. 'Why should it bother me? I'm sure you enjoyed your little joke.'

'There was no joke, Robyn,' he rasped harshly. 'Not on you or anyone else.'

'I'm sure there wasn't,' she scorned. 'We all go around masquerading as other people.'

'I told you why I did that.'

'To try and get into the part of your character Dominic,' she scoffed.

'I had no idea at the time how important you were going to become in my life——'

'Important!' she cut in. 'Spare me that—Mr Pendleton,' she took care not to call him Rick; she was determined never to call him that again. He would only take it as an invitation.

'But you are important to me. I admit I didn't want you to be, but that's the way it's worked out.'

'That's my cue to say I'm flattered,' Robyn said tautly, seeing with relief that they were nearing her home. 'Take it as said!' she snapped.

Instead of turning the car right, into her road, Rick veered the car off to the left instead, driving half a mile or so down the dirt-track before switching off the engine and turning in his seat to face her.

'What happens now?' She faced him unflinchingly.

'I kiss you and bring you to your senses,' he said grimly, moving dangerously towards her.

'If you kiss me——'

'You'll scream,' he finished dryly. 'I think you might have some trouble doing that with my mouth on yours. Besides, who would hear you out here?'

They were rather isolated—in fact, they were parked out in the middle of nowhere! She was at Rick's mercy!

'That's right,' he seemed to guess her thoughts. 'And you might as well get used to being kissed by me, it's going to happen a lot in future.'

She pushed ineffectually at the hard wall of his chest. 'You're arrogant, conceited——'

'And I *want* you,' he moaned, a hand either side of her face as he lowered his lips to hers.

She shouldn't be enjoying this, she *shouldn't*! But she was, the tears she had shed over him in the past now seemed unimportant. This was Rick, the man she loved, and she liked being held by him, kissed by him.

'Oh, Robyn, Robyn,' his lips travelled slowly across her cheek to nibble on the lobe of her ear. 'Relax, darling,' he encouraged softly. 'Let me love you.'

She didn't have the strength to stop him, her groan one of pleasure as he undid the buttons on her blouse, his mouth now moving to the firm curve of her breasts in the cream lacy bra.

She must be mad—this couldn't be happening to her here in broad daylight. Rick was making love to her, physically arousing her, and she was letting him, was even encouraging him as her hands became enmeshed in the thick dark vibrancy of his hair, holding him tightly to her.

His skin felt smooth and firm as he encouraged her hands under his sweat-shirt, gently pushing her back on the seat, his hard thrusting thighs on her as his mouth plundered hers with a thoroughness that left her head spinning.

Rick lifted his head, his eyes glazed with passion. 'You own me, Robyn,' he gasped, his face tense with the effort it took for him to control the quicksilver desire his body couldn't even begin to hide. 'I belong to you.' His kisses were heated against her throat.

He didn't belong to her at all, he belonged to Sheila! She

began to struggle, pushing his arms away, squirming away from those probing, arousing kisses. She sat up, buttoning her blouse with shaking fingers, blinking back the tears she wouldn't give him the satisfaction of seeing.

'You don't belong to anyone,' she told him vehemently. 'And in future I want you to just leave me alone. Go back to London, to your sophisticated friends, and just stay away from me!'

Rick shook his head. 'I can't do that, you and I both know I can't.'

'And what about your patients?' she snapped, smoothing her hair, knowing she hadn't managed to completely erase the devastation of his kisses, her lips still throbbing from his fierceness. 'Don't you owe loyalty to them if no one else?'

'I don't have any patients right now. When Melinda decided to leave me I took a year off to do what I wanted to do.' He shrugged. 'I still have six months left, six months during which I intend to pursue you.' His eyes deepened in colour. 'I'm going to marry you, Robyn.'

She gasped, going very white. 'And—and Sheila?'

He sighed. 'Until she marries again she'll continue to be my responsibility——'

'Responsibility?' Robyn echoed shrilly. 'My God, you're a bastard! Surely she means more than a responsibility to you? Don't you care about her at all?'

'Of course I care about her,' Rick rasped. 'But I have my own life to lead—she understands that.'

'Not with me you don't!' Robyn told him fiercely. 'I'll never marry you. Never!'

His expression darkened. 'I love you,' he groaned, his voice raw with the emotion.

Her breath caught in her throat, her eyes like shadowed violets as she stared at him. 'Wh—what did you say?' she gulped, sure she couldn't have heard him correctly. How could any man propose and tell a woman he loved her when he was already married!

Rick drew in a ragged breath. 'I love you. After the way Melinda walked out on me I didn't think I would ever get involved again, but you, with your open frankness, your beautiful body,' his gaze roamed slowly over her, as if he couldn't help himself, 'you've captured my heart in a way I never thought any woman would.'

Robyn shook her head, putting her hands over her ears. 'I don't want to hear any more of this,' she choked. 'Take me home. Please, take me home,' she pleaded.

'Robyn——'

'Please!' There was a sob in her voice.

'All right,' he agreed grimly. 'But this conversation is far from over.' He put the car into gear and backed down on to the main road.

His words were by way of being a warning, and Robyn shivered, carefully avoiding looking at his dark features as he concentrated on reversing the car. She licked her lips, aware that they felt bruised and sensitive from the pressure of Rick's. 'As far as I'm concerned,' she said in a voice that sounded totally unlike her own, 'this conversation was over ten minutes ago.'

'Before I kissed you and told you I love you, you mean,' he said harshly.

'Before you tried to seduce me with words as well as your body,' she corrected, anger in her voice now. 'Because that's all they were, words. And they came too late, much too late.'

'Because of Brian or Alan?'

She knew what he meant, and her cheeks flamed with colour. 'None of your damned business!' she snapped. 'Who I choose to sleep with has nothing to do with you.'

'If you told me it could save them both being beaten to a pulp when I try to find out which one of them has had you.'

Robyn gasped, a quiet determination in his voice telling her he meant to carry out this threat. 'You're crude! And you have a nerve, just thinking you can take over my life in this way. You have no right——'

'I have every right! You gave yourself to me the night of my accident——'

'I didn't know about Melinda then, or Sheila,' she interrupted accusingly.

'That's in my past,' he said angrily. 'I want you to be my future. The moment I met you I knew you meant trouble, with a capital T. You've thrown my life into disorder, got me so churned up that when I'm not with you I can't think of anything *but* you, and then when I'm with you I can't even think straight. I've met you late in my life——'

'Like I said, too late,' she put in stiffly.

'Not too late,' he rasped. 'Good God, girl, you weren't even alive half of my life. Of course there've been other women, but if I'd known, if I'd realised I was going to meet someone I could love so totally——'

'You would have stayed celibate!' she scorned.

'Strange as that may seem, yes,' he said huskily. 'I always thought sex was just sex, that as long as both partners were willing and it was enjoyable that was all there was to it. But compared with what I now feel for you I felt nothing for those other women, and going to bed with them was a waste of time. Just as going to bed with Brian or Alan was a waste of time for you.' He turned in his seat to look at her as he stopped the car outside her home, gently touching the hair at her nape. 'Which one was it, Robyn?'

Robyn flinched from him, hating him in that moment. 'Go to hell!' she stormed before slamming out of the car.

CHAPTER NINE

THE door of the shop closed forcibly behind her, making her father look up from his book-work. Robyn was breathing heavily, an angry glitter to her eyes.

'What's upset you?' her father asked gently.

'Nothing!' she snapped.

He smiled. 'Now I know you're upset. Still, I'd rather see you like this than with that long face you've had for weeks.'

'Dad——'

'All right, all right,' he held up protesting hands, 'I won't mention it any more. But it's nice to have the old Robyn back,' he added softly as she walked past him.

She swallowed hard. 'I'm sorry if I've been a pain, Dad, but I——' She broke off as the shop door opened, the bell ringing to warn of someone's entrance, and turned to see Rick just closing the door behind him. 'Excuse me,' she mumbled before hurriedly disappearing into the house at the back of the shop, her father's surprised expression the last thing she saw.

How dared Rick follow her into the shop! Why couldn't he get the message?—after all, she had made her feelings clear enough. But had she? Verbally her message had come across loud and clear, physically . . . Physically she had been as powerless to stop her mindless response as usual.

'You're nice and early, love. I haven't even—What's the matter with you?' her mother frowned at her as she entered the kitchen.

Robyn sighed. Did all her family know her so well! 'Nothing.'

Her mother raised her eyebrows. 'Somebody's upset you, that's for sure.'

'No one——' She sighed again. 'I'm not really very good company at the moment, Mum. I should have calmed down by the time I've washed and changed for dinner.'

But she hadn't. All the time she was upstairs she was fuming about the fact that Rick had actually followed her into the shop. Unless of course he had come in to buy something! Why hadn't she thought of that earlier? Some of the tension left her as she walked down the stairs.

Until she went into the lounge! Rick was in there, sitting quite at ease in one of the armchairs, a cup of tea resting on the arm.

'What are you doing here?' she demanded in a fierce whisper. Rick was alone in the room, her mother obviously busy in the kitchen getting the dinner.

'Drinking tea,' he replied calmly, completely relaxed, his long legs stretched out in front of him.

'You know what I——'

'Ah, Robyn,' her mother came in from the kitchen, a wide smile on her lips, 'I'm glad you've come down, I was just about to call you. Mr Howarth is here to see you.'

Robyn's couldn't meet her mother candid gaze. 'So I see,' she said tightly.

Her mother looked nonplussed, obviously surprised at Robyn's attitude towards the man she had been pining away for for the last two months. 'I—I think I forgot to put salt in the potatoes,' she said hastily. 'You like potatoes, I presume, Mr Howarth?'

'Rick, please,' he smiled. 'And I love potatoes. My waistline isn't too keen,' he shrugged, 'but I love them.'

'Go on with you!' Robyn's mother chuckled. 'You're in the peak of condition. I wish my Peter looked as fit.'

She went back to the kitchen, a smile still on her lips.

Robyn flashed Rick's lean body a resentful glance, indignant on her father's behalf. He couldn't help his thickening waistline, especially when her mother was such a good cook.

She frowned. 'What was that about the potatoes?'

Rick calmly took another sip of his tea. 'Your parents have kindly invited me to dinner.'

'They——! You didn't accept!'

'I did.'

'You—God, you—How could you!' she exploded.

'Quite easily,' he drawled, not at all perturbed by her anger. 'I happen to be hungry. I didn't get any lunch today,' he added pointedly.

'But you—you can't eat here,' she said in exasperation.

He shrugged. 'I've already accepted.'

Robyn almost stamped her foot with frustration. 'Then you can just unaccept!'

'Why?'

'Why?' she blinked. 'Because I—I don't want you here.'

'That's a pity, because I have no intention of leaving.' He placed his empty cup on the table, relaxing back in the seat once again.

'But you must!' She marched over to him and tried to pull him out of the chair. 'You have to go!' She tugged on his arm, but made no impression. 'Rick, you——'

'Ah, at last,' he sighed his satisfaction, pulling her down to sit on his knee, his lips on her throat. 'We're friends again, hmm?'

'No, we're not!' She pummelled her fists against his shoulders. 'I only called you Rick because——'

'Because that's my name and you love me,' he murmured against her satiny skin.

'I do not! And that isn't your name—Mr Pendleton.'

'Ah, ah, naughty, naughty,' he shook his head. 'You deserve punishment for that.'

Her 'punishment' took the form of his lips moving persuasively on hers, forcing her to the back of the chair as he deepened the kiss.

Robyn felt as if she couldn't breathe, struggling against this seduction for all she was worth. He was Oliver Pendleton, Oliver Pendleton! She kept repeating it to herself over and over again—it was the only way she could hold herself aloof from him.

He at last raised his head, his eyes a warm glowing grey, a complete contrast to the first time she had met him; his harshness had surrounded him like a cloak then. 'Not ready to give in yet?' he murmured.

'Never!' Her eyes flashed violet.

'Robyn——'

'Hey, Mum, I—Oh!' Billy went silent.

Robyn turned an embarrassed face to her brother, seeing his own discomfort as he looked at her sitting on Rick's knee. She pushed against Rick's arms about her waist, his fingers refusing to be pried away.

She licked her lips, giving up the fight, and instantly felt the pressure removed, allowing her to stand up. She ran damp palms down her denim-clad thighs. 'H—Hello, Billy.' Her eyes shifted from him nervously.

'Hello, Sis. Sir,' he looked at Rick.

Rick stood up too, instantly dwarfing both Robyn and Billy. 'I don't think I've thanked you yet for your prompt action the night of my accident,' he spoke to Billy, shaking his hand. 'And I do thank you.'

'That's all right,' Billy shrugged it off with boyish modesty. 'Dealing with you was quite easy compared to dealing with Robyn!'

Enquiring grey eyes were turned on her. 'Dealing with Robyn . . .?' he prompted Billy.

The young boy grinned. 'You should have seen her. She——'

'That's enough, Billy,' she cut in warningly. 'Mr Howarth isn't interested in that now.'

Rick crossed his arms in front of his chest. 'Oh, but I am,' he smiled. 'I'm very interested.'

'Well, it will have to keep for another time,' she said briskly, promising herself that she would warn Billy later to guard his tongue in future. She wasn't proud of her actions the night of Rick's accident, not any of them. 'Go and wash up for dinner now,' she ordered her brother.

'I hate bossy sisters,' he muttered to Rick.

He grinned. 'How many sisters do you have?'

Billy grimaced. 'Just the one. She's enough.'

'Billy!' she warned once again.

He sighed. 'You see what I mean?' He shook his head, going up the stairs.

'So,' Rick turned to face her, his arms going about her waist to link his hands at the base of her spine, bringing their thighs close together. 'What did your brother mean just now?'

Her mouth set stubbornly. 'He didn't mean anything,' she mumbled, avoiding his eyes.

'Oh, but he did.'

'No! He——'

'Well, that's the shop shut up,' her father said as he came into the room, showing no surprise at seeing his only daughter in the arms of a man he barely knew. He sat down. 'If you have to do that do you think you could move over a little?' he requested. 'I'd like to watch the news.'

Rick grinned. 'Certainly.' He gently pushed Robyn away from standing in front of the television. 'You were saying?' he prompted softly.

'No, I wasn't,' she snapped, looking selfconsciously

at her father. He didn't appear to be taking any notice of them, his attention on the television set he had switched on. 'Let me go!' she hissed at Rick.

He shook his head. 'Not until you tell me what happened to you on the night of my accident.' His tone was adamant.

So was hers! 'I will not!'

He shrugged. 'Then you stay here.'

'You're just about the most high-handed, overbearing——' Robyn broke off as she heard her father chuckling at them. 'It isn't funny!' she stormed angrily.

'Isn't it?' he asked mildly. 'From where I'm sitting it's very funny. Talk about the pot calling the kettle black . . .'

'I'm not like that,' she said indignantly, turning to glare at Rick as he too began to laugh. 'I'm not!' she insisted angrily.

'You are, love,' her father grinned. 'And I take full responsibility for it. But I should tell Mr Howarth what he wants to know, he looks as if he could hold out longer than you.'

Rick did indeed look very comfortable, his hands still linked at the base of her spine, effectively moulding her curves to the hardness of his.

'I'm not telling him anything,' Robyn said childishly, turning her head away from the mockery in his dancing grey eyes.

Her father tutted. 'Perhaps you should ask me, son,' he sighed. 'Robyn's in one of her uncommunicative moods.'

'I didn't know she had them,' Rick grinned. 'Usually I have trouble shutting her up.'

'Ooh——'

'See?' he shrugged at her father.

'Mm,' her father nodded. 'You do seem to have that effect on her. So what was it you wanted to know?' he listened as Rick told him. 'Oh, that,' he said dismissively.

'I can tell you that. Robyn——'

'Dad!' she said fiercely, glaring at him. 'Dad, please,' she added pleadingly.

He quirked one eyebrow. 'You don't want him to know, hmm?'

She closed her eyes. 'No.'

He shrugged. 'Then that's that. Sorry, Rick, but I have to live with her. She can be pretty impossible at times.'

'Dad!' she groaned her embarrassment.

What Rick would have said then she had no way of knowing, as her mother called them in to dinner at that moment, and Rick at last released her. But not before her mother had also seen her held firmly in his arms! It was as if he were staking his claim in front of her whole family. And he had no right to!

But she was strangely reluctant to tell them of his married status, finding it enjoyable, when not in the torture of his embrace, to have him here with her family. It was a stolen moment of his company, one that couldn't possibly hurt Sheila.

Considering the sort of life he must lead when in London he fitted in remarkably well with her family, talking business with her father, complimenting her mother on her cooking, and talking extensively to Billy about football, a subject he seemed to know a lot about, surprisingly.

By the end of the meal Robyn knew that Rick had been a success with everyone, and the looks of warm possession he kept giving her made her blush with pleasure. If only he weren't married then everything would have been perfect.

Shortly after ten he stood up to leave, looking more relaxed and at ease than Robyn had ever seen him.

Her father stood up to shake his hand. 'Nice to have had the opportunity of meeting you properly.'

Rick grasped his hand warmly. 'I'm afraid my manners weren't at their best the last time I saw you.'

Robyn's father shook his head. 'I understood. And I don't think Robyn helped,' he added teasingly. 'I think she was annoying you even then. No respect for the fact that you shouldn't hit a man when he's down.'

'I didn't hit him!' her eyes sparkled angrily. 'As I remember it he—he——'

'I kissed her,' Rick finished dryly. 'But only to shut her up.'

Her father nodded. 'I remember. It worked too. You have quite a drive in front of you now, don't you?' He changed the subject as he saw Robyn was becoming increasingly agitated.

'You could always stay the night here,' her mother put in. 'If you don't mind sharing with Billy.'

'I appreciate your offer,' Rick said warmly. 'But I don't have a long drive, in fact I'm only going down the road.'

Robyn went pale, staring at him dazedly. 'Down the road . . .?'

He nodded. 'To Orchard House.'

She licked her dry lips. 'You're staying there again?'

'I'm living there,' he corrected. 'I bought it.'

She swallowed hard. 'Bought it . . .?' she repeated disbelievingly.

He nodded, smiling his satisfaction. 'That's right. I now live at Orchard House.'

'But I—There's no furniture or—or anything,' she said desperately.

'There is now. You'll have to come down and see the changes I've made,' he invited huskily.

'That would be nice, wouldn't it, dear?' her mother said warmly.

'Lovely,' Robyn agreed with not a trace of sincerity in her voice. 'But you can't even cook for yourself,' she pointed out to Rick. 'Or do you have a housekeeper?'

'No,' he shook his head. 'But I'm working on getting someone in to take care of me very soon.' The look in his eyes left no one in any doubt *who* he was intending it to be.

Robyn saw the look her parents exchanged, and blushed deeply red. 'I'll see you to the door,' she told Rick tightly, edging him out of the room.

'If you're on your own,' her mother spoke before she managed to get him out, 'perhaps you would like to come to lunch on Sunday?'

Robyn groaned inwardly, further annoyed by mockery in deep grey eyes. Oh, he was enjoying this!

'I'd love to,' he instantly accepted.

'Lovely,' her mother beamed. 'About one o'clock?'

'I'll be here,' he promised, at last allowing Robyn to manoeuvre him out into the hallway. 'Something wrong?' he quirked a mocking eyebrow at her furious expression.

'You know there is,' she said forcefully. 'I don't want you to come here to lunch on Sunday or any other day,' she told him rudely.

'Too bad, the invitation didn't come from you.'

'I wouldn't have invited you!'

His mouth twisted. 'I know that. Ignoring me isn't going to make me go away, Robyn.'

'I wish you would!'

'Liar!' he chuckled.

'You think you're so clever, don't you?' she glared at him. 'You force your way into my home——'

Rick shook his head. 'There was no force about it. I came into the shop to give you this,' he held up her purse, 'and your father invited me to dinner.'

'My purse . . .' she groaned as she took it out of his hand.

'Yes, you ungrateful little wretch. Wasn't that worth dinner?'

'I—No! Yes,' she admitted reluctantly. 'But it isn't worth lunch too,' she added with rebellion.

'I've already accepted,' he shrugged. 'And I don't intend unaccepting.'

'I'll make sure I'm out,' she said childishly.

'Then I'll have a nice chat with your parents instead.'

Her eyes widened. 'You wouldn't?'

Rick quirked one eyebrow. 'Want to take the chance?'

Robyn bit her lip. 'You know I don't.'

He bent to kiss her hard on the mouth. 'I'll see you on Sunday—unless I see you before.'

'You won't,' she insisted firmly.

'We'll see.'

His words were in the form of a threat, and Robyn was determined to see him thwarted.

Selma was ecstatic about her date the next day. Alan apparently lived up to all her expectations. 'He's so—so nice,' she said with feeling. 'We went for a drink after the cinema.'

The evening must have been a success for Alan too, then. After all, he hadn't had to take Selma out for a drink. 'I'm glad you had a good time,' Robyn smiled, looking a little pale, mainly due to a disturbed night's sleep.

She was utterly confused herself. Rick loved her, wanted to marry her, and she knew she loved him in return, but she baulked at his married status. Not that she would be the first girl to fall in love with a married man, far from it, and she wouldn't be the first girl to have to wait to marry that man while he attained a divorce either. But she knew she just couldn't do it, she couldn't take her happiness at the expense of someone else's.

'It was more than good,' Selma said dreamily. 'Alan is so different from everyone else I've ever been out with. He actually talks to me!'

Robyn frowned. 'You mean your other boy-friends didn't?'

'Not like Alan does,' Selma shook her head. 'He really talks to me, treats me as an intelligent equal.'

'But you are.' She knew that Selma was highly qualified for this job.

'I know,' Selma sighed. 'But most boys prefer to think of girls as a little on the stupid side. All the ones I've been out with seem to, anyway. I've always found it easier to act the way they expect me to than compete with them,' she added with a grimace.

'That's terrible,' Robyn exclaimed.

Selma shrugged. 'That's life.'

'No man is going to make me act like that,' Robyn declared with certainty.

Selma gave her a sideways glance. 'Even if that someone was Rick?' she teased.

'He would never treat me like that.' And she knew he wouldn't. He treated her as an equal, someone with intelligence and humour.

'He's really wonderful,' Selma smiled. 'And the way he looks at you! I've never seen anyone devour another person with their eyes before.'

'Selma!' Robyn groaned.

'Well, he did,' she grinned. 'I felt quite envious.'

'You're welcome to him—if you like married men, that is,' she revealed tightly.

Selma's eyes widened. 'Married? Is he?'

'Yes.'

'That's a shame,' she sighed. 'You were quite keen on him, weren't you?'

She was more than 'keen' on him, and it was a disaster, not a *shame*. 'Not any more,' she lied. 'Tell me more about you and Alan. Are you seeing him again?'

'Tomorrow,' the other girl confirmed. 'He's taking me to a football match, of all things.'

And it didn't need two guesses why! Alan still didn't trust Selma's interest in him, was taking her to watch a sporting event to show her that he could no longer compete but had to stand on the sidelines.

Robyn mentioned it to him later. 'Don't you think you're being rather persistent about it?' she queried gently.

'No.' His expression was harsh.

'Well, I think you are. Selma is so pleased that you see her as a person and not just a sex object that I don't think she's even given the fact that you used to be an athlete a thought.'

'Exactly. I want her to think about it, to realise——'

'You're always talking about roles, Alan,' she cut in angrily. 'Well, right now you're stuck in a groove of self-pity. Oh yes, you are,' she insisted as he went to protest. 'Selma doesn't give a damn about whether or not you can still run a four-minute mile, or whatever.'

'Four-minute!' he scoffed. 'You're a little out of touch, Robyn. It's a little faster than that now.'

'You see? I bet Selma is no more informed about things like that than I am.'

'Wrong.'

'Wrong?'

'Yes,' Alan nodded. 'She knows so much about a lot of things. Are you going down to the baker's?' he asked briskly. 'You are? Well, I'll walk down with you and we can talk while we walk.'

Robyn raised her eyes heavenwards. 'A poet and he doesn't know it!' She picked up her handbag in preparation of leaving to go and collect her lunch. 'Come on, I'll buy you a cheese roll,' she joked.

'Ham.'

She grinned. 'All right, ham.'

Alan smiled as they left by the back door. 'I think I like having lunch with you.'

'I'll bet.' She turned to smile at him. 'You can buy me lunch tomorrow.'

'It's your half-day.'

'All right, Saturday.'

'Robyn . . .'

Oh no! She was almost afraid to turn around. Rick was here again, and by the look of the haughty arrogance in his face he didn't appreciate her being with Alan. Well, damn him, she would have lunch with whom she pleased! She didn't have to answer to him for any of her movements.

She looked up at him with unflinching eyes, as usual her heart giving a painful jolt just at the sight of him. He was casually dressed again, light denims and a partly unbuttoned shirt, noticeably free of creases today. He looked very dark and virile, not the part of Oliver Pendleton at all.

'I've come to take you to lunch,' he said before she could speak.

She felt Alan's hand on her arm. 'I'm sorry,' she refused huskily. 'I already have a lunch date.' Thank God Alan had realised this was the man she needed his protection against!

A look of irritation crossed Rick's face before his attention was transferred to Alan, his eyes glacial. 'Would you take your hands off my fiancée?' he snapped tautly.

Robyn gasped. 'But I'm not——'

Rick pulled her to his side. 'I'm sure Mr.—Alan understands that I have first claim on your time.'

Alan looked at her searchingly, seeing her white, shocked features. 'I would say Robyn is capable of choosing for herself.' He wasn't in the least intimidated by the other man's attitude. 'Robyn?'

She moved closer to him. 'I'm having lunch with Alan,' she told Rick defensively. 'But my parents are still expecting you for lunch on Sunday,' she added at the dangerous glitter in his eyes.

His stance was challenging. 'Are you going to be there?'

She licked her lips. 'I—I—Yes.'

He nodded. 'I'll see you then.' He turned on his heel and walked towards the Rolls parked a short distance away.

Alan heaved a sigh of relief, watching as the car moved off smoothly down the road. 'If he'd decided to fight me for you I think I might have lost,' he admitted ruefully.

Robyn moved shakily. 'Of course you wouldn't,' she dismissed briskly, knowing even as she said it that she lied. Rick was as muscular as Alan, plus he had been motivated by anger, and in that sort of mood he could take on anyone and win.

'I wouldn't bet on it.' Alan removed his arm from about her waist. 'Just who is he?'

She bit her lip and started to walk on again, although she had no appetite for lunch now. 'I told you, he's just someone I don't want to get involved with.'

'With a Rolls?'

'A car isn't everything!' she flashed.

Alan shrugged. 'He looked as if he had quite a lot else going for him too.'

'Well, he doesn't!' She walked off angrily.

'Hey!' Alan caught her up several minutes later. 'Okay, okay, so you aren't interested in the man.'

'I'm not!'

'Then why are you so angry?'

'Because—because——'

'Because you really like him,' Alan finished. 'I'm sorry, Robyn,' he said at her furious glance, 'but you gave me some plain speaking a few minutes ago, now I'm giving you some. If you like the man, and he obviously likes you, why do you keep fighting him?'

'I already told you, he's married.'

Alan sighed. 'I hate to spoil any of your girlish dreams, but not all marriages are made in heaven. His has obviously broken down.'

'And I'm not going to help it come to an end,' she said fiercely.

'Okay,' he shrugged, 'I won't mention it again.'

'I'd appreciate it!'

She didn't see Rick again until Sunday, no calling for her at lunchtime, and no collecting her from work. After Thursday she hadn't really been surprised, and yet there was a certain amount of disappointment. It was ridiculous to feel that way, and yet she did, glaring her resentment at him as soon as he came into the room at exactly one o'clock, her mother enthusing over the flowers he had bought her.

'Robyn,' he greeted tersely, sitting down when her father invited him to do so.

'Ri—er—Hello,' she returned huskily.

His mouth twisted as she avoided calling him Rick. 'You haven't been over to see the changes at Orchard House.'

'No, I——' her hands moved nervously together as she paced the room, 'I haven't had the time,' she couldn't meet his eyes.

'Maybe you could walk back with Rick this afternoon,' her mother suggested.

'I——'

'What a good idea,' Rick interrupted her refusal. 'I'd like you to see the—house, Robyn.'

'I—Oh, very well,' she agreed ungraciously.

Rick was like the cat that had swallowed the cream

all through lunch, getting on with her family just as well as he had the last time.

'Robyn and I will wash the dishes,' he offered as they cleared away the debris from the meal.

'I can do it alone,' she said stiffly. 'You go and—and talk to my parents.'

'I'm sure you would rather I helped you,' he said deeply, his tone warning.

'I—Yes. Yes, perhaps that would be best.' She marched angrily through to the kitchen, knowing that he followed her, aware of his every move without even looking at him.

She knew he was standing directly behind her now, could feel his warm breath on her nape. But she didn't turn, but continued to wash the dishes as if her life depended on it, her whole body tense.

His lips brushed lightly against her neck, his arms moving about her waist as he pulled her back against him. 'I love you,' he groaned into her throat.

Robyn pulled away from him, spinning round. 'Stop that,' she cried. 'Just stop it!'

'But I can't,' he held his hands up defensively. 'I love you, I want to marry you.'

Her mouth set in an angry line. 'If you don't stop this I'm going to tell my parents about you!'

He took hold of her hand. 'That's a good idea—why don't we both tell them?' He pulled her in the direction of the lounge; her mother and father were in there, although Billy had gone out with one of his friends. 'Come on, Robyn,' Rick smiled confidently.

She hung back. 'Are you mad?'

'Madly in love, yes.'

She came to a halt. 'Rick, don't do this. Leave now and we can just forget the whole thing.'

'Not on your life, especially now that you've called me Rick.'

Robyn didn't fight him any longer, but allowed herself to be led into the lounge. Her parents had to know the truth about Rick some time, so why not now?

Rick didn't hesitate for a moment. 'Mr Castle, I would like your permission to marry your daughter,' he announced.

Robyn swallowed hard, shocked by the starkness of his statement. She hadn't expected him to be quite so blunt.

'I love her,' he continued. 'And I believe she loves me, although she won't admit to it——'

'And you know why!' she rounded on him angrily, knowing that her parents were surprised by this sudden turn of events. She doubted they had been expecting Rick to propose in front of them this way. She hadn't either! 'I've had enough of this, Rick,' she tugged her hand free of this. 'I think I should tell my parents who you are and——'

'They have a right to know that,' he shrugged. 'My name isn't Rick Howarth,' he told them candidly.

'He's Oliver Pendleton,' she inserted pointedly.

'Okay,' he sighed, shooting her an impatient glance, 'it's Oliver Pendleton. If that's what's bothering you——'

'It isn't,' she said tightly, wishing this confrontation didn't have to come in front of her parents. But Rick had wanted it this way. 'It's the fact that you're already married that does that.'

'Married?' her father gasped. 'I don't understand any of this. I don't understand why you're here under an assumed name, Mr Howarth——er——Pendleton——'

'My name is Rick, and it isn't assumed,' he said tightly, not taking his eyes off Robyn. 'Robyn, what the hell are you talking about?' he rasped.

'You know what!'

'If it isn't assumed,' her father persisted, 'how can

you be both Rick Howarth and Oliver Pendleton?'

'Oliver Richard Howarth Pendleton,' Robyn supplied vaguely. 'Don't pretend any more, Rick,' she pleaded.

'I'm not pretending,' he snapped. 'And I want an explanation.'

She heaved a heavy sigh. 'I met Sheila, remember?'

'So?' he frowned.

'She's your wife!'

His face darkened furiously. 'Like hell she is!' he exploded. 'She's my brother's wife.'

Robyn gasped, her face very white. 'Your sister-in-law?'

'Yes,' he snapped.

'But I don't understand. I—Your brother, he wasn't at the party.'

'What party?' her father cut in.

'He wasn't there,' Rick told her savagely, 'because he's dead. He and Melinda were killed in a car crash.'

'Melinda?' Robyn's father was totally confused now.

'I'll explain later, Dad,' Robyn dismissed, confused herself. 'He's the doctor Melinda ran away with?' she asked Rick dazedly.

'Yes,' he confirmed tautly.

'Then I—Oh God, what have I done!' she groaned, seeing the dislike on Rick's face. And no wonder! 'Rick, I——'

'You really thought me capable of asking you to marry me while I was married to Sheila?' he demanded.

'I—I thought——'

'You thought altogether too damned much,' he scorned harshly. 'Consider my marriage offer withdrawn,' he strode angrily to the door, turning to shake his head. 'I don't think I ever knew you, Robyn, and now I don't think I want to.' He quietly closed the door as he left.

CHAPTER TEN

ROBYN wanted to run after him, to beg his forgiveness, but the disgust in his face held her back. He hated her now, she had seen it in his eyes, and she couldn't really blame him for feeling that way.

Besides, by the time she had finished answering her parents' questions it was much too late to run after Rick. She had made a complete mess of everything, had jumped to conclusions when she should have realised Rick would never behave that way, he was much too forthright and honest. And now she had destroyed his love with her own distrust.

She had never felt so miserable, even more so because her parents were disgusted with her behaviour, sympathising completely with Rick.

Robyn went for a walk that evening, her footsteps taking her past Orchard House. The Rolls was parked outside, but the house itself was in darkness. She stood outside for what seemed like hours, but there was no sign of movement inside. She finally had to go home, not brave enough to go to the door and face Rick's anger.

She didn't sleep, she couldn't relax enough for that, and the next week progressed the same way. She did her work, she went home, she even made a token show of eating, and then she would go to bed ... The nights were the worst, long black nights that stretched out in front of her like an endless void.

She went to work heavy-eyed and exhausted, although her work wasn't suffering at all. And while she was the most miserable she had ever been in her life Selma and

Alan's romance seemed to be blossoming. The other couple spent most of their time together now, although Alan still seemed to have reservations about the relationship.

'You can't fall in love that quickly,' he told Robyn during a coffee-break together.

You could fall in love at a glance, she knew that. 'Do you love Selma?' she asked him.

He looked away. 'I—I'm not sure.'

'Does she love you?'

He grimaced. 'She says she does.'

'If she says she does then she does. Selma doesn't lie.'

'But——'

'For God's sake, Alan,' she snapped angrily, 'accept what you've got, and don't throw love away like I did.'

He frowned. 'That man——'

'Yes!' she hissed. 'I've lost him, because I was stupid, as you're being.'

He looked uncertain. 'I don't know——'

She stood up forcefully. 'You're stupid, stupid and—and proud. And that pride won't make you a very good companion for the rest of your life. Think about that!' She slammed out of the staff-room.

Selma was just coming up the stairs. 'What's all the noise about?' she asked in a whisper. 'You can be heard downstairs.'

Robyn glared at her. 'Ask your boy-friend!' She didn't attempt to lower her voice.

Selma looked startled. 'Alan? But——'

'He's up there.' Robyn jerked her head in the direction of the staff-room. 'It's about time the two of you came to your senses.'

'Robyn——'

'Excuse me,' and Selma pushed past the other girl, clattering down the stairs.

Mr Leaven was waiting for her. 'Was that you making

all that noise, Miss Castle?' he asked sternly.

Robyn's head went back, her anger a tangible thing. 'Yes, it was,' she told him firmly.

'Oh.' For once he seemed to be unsure of his own reaction. 'I—Well, make sure it doesn't happen again,' he muttered before returning to his desk.

The anger instantly left her. She was just so tired, she wanted Rick so much, and she knew that he had put her firmly out of his life.

No one in her family had seen or heard from him since last Sunday. He hadn't been into the shop, and he hadn't been seen about the village either. Robyn walked past the house most evenings, and each night it was the same, the Rolls parked outside but no sign of life inside the house.

She was glad when it was time to go home that evening, inwardly groaning when Alan and Selma joined her in the staff-room. It was too much to hope that she could escape without further reference to this morning.

'You're right, Robyn,' Alan said softly. 'I have been behaving stupidly.' His arm was about Selma's shoulders. 'We may not land up together, but we know that we love each other here and now.'

'I'm glad,' she said, and meant it, sure that this couple would indeed 'land up together'.

The bright sunshine outside did nothing to alleviate her own mood of depression as she walked to the bus-stop with her head down, her bicycle once more off the road.

She was so intent on the pavement that she walked straight into the person walking along in the opposite direction. 'I—Brian!' Her eyes widened with recognition.

'None other,' he grinned.

She frowned. 'You don't seem surprised to see me.'

'I'm not.' He took hold of her arm. 'I've come to give you a lift home.'

Robyn let him bundle her into his low sports car. 'But I——' she turned to face him as he climbed in beside her. 'How are you here?' she asked dazedly.

He glanced sideways at her as he moved the car out into the traffic. 'The how is obvious.' He looked pointedly at the car. 'It's the why that's going to take a little explaining.'

'All right,' she nodded. 'Why?'

Brian grimaced. 'I had a feeling you would say that.'

'Well?' she prompted.

'Patience,' he sighed. 'Did no one ever tell you it's a virtue?'

Her mouth twisted. 'Not that I can ever remember, no.'

'Then maybe they should have done. Okay,' he grinned at her impatience, 'I'm here visiting my aunt and uncle, so I called round to see Oliver.'

Robyn swallowed hard, looking down at her hands. 'How——' she cleared her throat, 'how is he?'

'Physically or mentally?'

'And you say you don't want to be a doctor!'

'I don't. And I'm not going to be. I like drama school.' He grinned. 'I like some of the girls even better.'

She quirked an eyebrow. 'And what does Trudi think of that?'

He frowned. 'Who? Oh—oh, Trudi,' he dismissed. 'We finished ages ago. It's Amy now.'

Robyn's mouth twisted. 'I'm glad I didn't cause any lasting damage to your heart! It's all right,' she spluttered with laughter at his woebegone expression, 'I was only teasing.'

'Well, don't—I was very fond of you. I still am, which is why I think you and Oliver should try and sort yourselves out.'

She looked away. 'There's nothing to sort out.'

'I happen to think there is. And to prove it . . .' he drove straight past the shop, turning into the driveway of Orchard House, 'I'm going to deposit you on Oliver's doorstep.' He parked the car outside the house.

She shook her head. 'It won't do any good.'

'On the contrary,' he got out, pulling her with him, 'it will make you face each other.'

'That won't do any good either,' she said tightly. 'He doesn't want to see me.'

'That's all you know,' Brian scorned. 'Believe me, he wants to see you—even if he doesn't realise it.' He knocked firmly on the door.

Robyn hung back. 'Oh, Brian, I——' She broke off as the door was wrenched open, to reveal a darkly scowling Rick standing in the doorway. He looked as unhappy as she did! 'Oh, Rick!' she choked.

Brian frowned. 'I don't know who Rick is, but I've bought you a present, Oliver.' He pushed Robyn towards the other man before striding back to his car, accelerating away with a wave of his hand. 'Invite me to the wedding.'

How had Selma described it, 'devouring her with his eyes'? Yes, that was it, and he was doing it again now. 'Oh, Rick,' she breathed raggedly, 'I love you. I love you so!' She took a tentative step towards him.

He met her half way, pulling her so tightly into his arms she thought he would squeeze all the breath out of her. 'I love you too, you crazy mixed-up child,' he groaned into her throat. 'I've been wanting all week to come and apologise,' he punctuated each word with a kiss, his lips fevered over her glowing love-drugged features.

'*You* apologise?' She pulled back to see his face, seeing only love there, all the love she could ever want or need. 'I was the one who didn't trust you, who——'

'How could you trust me?' he interrupted, taking her

inside the house and closing the door, instantly pulling her back into his arms. 'I'd never told you anything about myself accept that I wanted you, even my name wasn't really my name. And yet still you loved me, you brave darling. I went down to the shop this morning and had a long talk with your parents,' he added softly.

'You did?' her eyes were wide.

'I did,' he nodded. 'I couldn't take being away from you any longer. I asked their permission to marry you.'

'And?' she asked excitedly.

He shrugged. 'They said yes—if you'll have me. I was coming round this evening to ask you if you will. Will you?'

'Oh yes!' She threw herself into his waiting arms.

Rick hugged her tight. 'If you only knew how much I love you,' he groaned, his eyes almost black.

'If it's half as much as I love you it will do for me.'

'It's more, Robyn,' he told her seriously. 'Much, much more.'

She swallowed hard with the enormity of what he was saying. 'You love me more than you loved Melinda.' It was a statement, not a question.

'I was fond of Melinda, Robyn,' he said slowly. 'But I never loved her. She was beautiful, and I thought she would make me a good wife, but I never loved her. I didn't even know what love was until I met an impudent little witch whose honesty completely unnerves me.'

'Shall I be honest now?' she asked teasingly, the memory of Melinda firmly dismissed from her mind.

Rick smiled. 'I don't think you'd better. I can tell by the look in your eyes that you're going to say something you shouldn't.'

'I want to go to bed with you. Now.'

'You see?' he moaned. 'You can wait until we're married, young lady.'

'Can you?'

'I shall have to. No——' he stopped her talking by placing his lips on hers, 'I want you to be my wife first. I don't want anything to spoil it for you.'

The dinner had been a success—the steak, the wine, the candles on the table, that ridiculous concoction she had made for dessert because Rick had a sweet tooth. Their first wedding anniversary. One whole year spent together as man and wife.

It couldn't have been better. Their wedding night had been unspoilt, as Rick had wanted it. He was working in London during the week now, but most weekends they spent at Orchard House.

They sat before the log fire, its glow the only light in the room, Rick's arm about Robyn's shoulders, his lips nuzzling her throat. 'I have a present for you,' he murmured against her ear.

'Rick!' She squirmed with pleasure as his tongue traced the shell-like curve. 'You're insatiable!' Her meal had been delayed this evening because he preferred to go to bed instead of eating. 'Behave yourself,' she said sternly, knowing that it wouldn't be long before he carried her upstairs to bed and made love to her, their two bodies entwined in perfect harmony.

He raised his head, laughing softly. 'Not that sort of present,' he chuckled. 'It's an anniversary present.'

'But you already gave me this.' She touched the slender diamond bracelet he had given her during the meal.

'This isn't really a present.' He stood up, moving to take something out of his briefcase in the study. 'Here,' he came back and handed it to her.

'Your book!' Her eyes glowed with pride.

'The first copy from the publishers,' he nodded, pouring them both a glass of the champagne he had produced after their meal. 'Read the dedication,' he urged huskily.

She turned to the appropriate page, reading to herself. 'To Robyn, without whom this book couldn't have been written, without whom I wouldn't want to be alive'. She swallowed down the tears, knowing that meeting her had changed the whole character of this book. Dominic, the main character, was originally going to be allowed to die, but after Rick had met her he said that he couldn't let that happen, that if Dominic loved Barbara as much as he loved her, Robyn, then he would take any chance he had of being with her for always. What had started out as a tragedy had turned into a tender love story.

'Darling!' She launched herself into Rick's arms, more moved than she could ever tell him. 'It's beautiful!'

'So are you.' He held her tightly to him for several minutes, finally putting her away from him with a grin. 'Now I want to know what *did* happen the night of my accident. Your family seem to have clammed up about it. So out with it, woman.'

'I—I fainted,' she revealed reluctantly.

Triumph shone in his eyes. 'You did?'

'Yes, I did,' she said crossly. 'And you needn't look so pleased about it. I—I thought you were dead.'

'My poor darling!' He kissed away the frown from her brow.

She licked her lips nervously. 'Rick, I—I have a present for you too.'

'Dinner was enough. And these beautiful gold cuff-links you gave me—you didn't have to buy me anything else.'

Robyn bit her lip. 'Well, I didn't exactly *buy* this present, and you can't exactly have it *just* yet.'

Rick frowned, handing her her glass of champagne. 'Drink some more of this, darling, you aren't making much sense as it is.'

She sipped the champagne to give her confidence.

'Rick, I'm going to have your baby! Oh dear,' she sighed, 'I didn't mean it to come out quite as bluntly as that.' She looked at him anxiously.

Her husband had gone very pale. 'You—you're having a baby?' he repeated in a strangulated voice.

'Yes,' she nodded.

'Then what are you doing drinking alcohol?' He took the glass out of her hand. 'And you shouldn't have been working so hard today. How do you feel?' he asked anxiously, her hand held tightly in his.

Robyn spluttered with laughter at the near panic in his face. 'How many babies did you say you've brought into the world?'

'Hundreds,' he dismissed impatiently. 'But none of them were my own. God, are you all right, Robyn?'

'Of course I'm all right, I still have seven months to go yet. Rick, you aren't taking this at all as I expected you to. I thought you would be blasé about it, and I—I'm so excited myself!'

He gave her a reproachful look. 'You thought I would be *blasé* about your carrying our child?'

'Well—yes,' she admitted reluctantly.

'Well, I'm not. I'm excited too, overjoyed, ecstatic. I can't describe how proud I feel of you.' He frowned suddenly. 'Do you want me to be with you at the birth?'

She smiled. 'Well, it would be nice, you are the expert, after all.'

'Mm,' he mused. 'I wonder how it would look for the expert to have passed out on the floor?'

'You surely aren't squeamish——'

'Only because it's you, darling.' His arms tightened about her protectively. 'If anything happened to you . . .! I couldn't bear it,' he shuddered.

'Nothing is going to happen to me,' she gently reassured him, basking in the love her husband wasn't ashamed to tell the whole world.

And nothing did happen to her. Théir daughter was born perfectly normally, an instant hit with her father from the start, her blonde downy hair just like Robyn's, her eyes the lightest of blue, looking as if they might later be the deep grey of her father's.

Harlequin® Plus

HISTORY OF THE BICYCLE

A bicycle? Why it's nothing more than a light, two-wheeled, steerable vehicle propelled by human power. But tell that to Robyn, Carole Mortimer's heroine, as she pedals her trusty bike through the streets of her little English village. For doubtless she truly appreciates this vehicle for what it actually is: an efficient and very inexpensive form of transportation.

Bicycles have been used around the world by millions of people for more than a century. The forerunner of the cycle we know today was invented by a Scotsman, Kirkpatrick Macmillan, in 1839. He was also the first person to race on one. While sipping a pint in a Glasgow pub, he wagered a coachdriver friend that he could reach the nearby town of Sanqhar before the coach did. The two set off and were neck and neck for several miles before the cyclist won. Of course, Macmillan didn't have to stop for the mail as the coach did!

A few years passed before the bicycle became practical for most people to ride. Early models were called "boneshakers," and later came the well-known "penny-farthing" with its tiny rear wheel and enormous front wheel. By 1893 the bicycle design known today came into use—and its popularity hasn't stopped growing.

In Europe it has long been common for people to rely on bicycles instead of cars to get to work. In the past decade the bicycle trend has caught on in North America, too, as people try to beat the energy crisis—and stay physically fit!

Take these 4 best-selling novels FREE